THE SEARCH FOR MIRI

A PROFOUND ADVENTURE OF FAITH

FRANK D. TIGUE

THE SEARCH FOR MIRI

A PROFOUND ADVENTURE OF FAITH

FRANK D. TIGUE

ISBN: 978-1-967375-54-7 (Paperback)

ISBN: 978-1-967375-55-4 (E-book)

Library of Congress Control Number: 2025915162

Printed in the United States of America

Published by:

info@thequippyquill.com
(302) 295-2278

Dedication

To Elizabeth Lay, without her encouragement and her anticipation of reading more (since she gave the thumbs up to everything I wrote and desired me to continue), this book would not have been possible. To her, I proudly dedicate this book.

Contents

CHAPTER 1

The Apparition from the Mist

I do not know how long I had been walking. However, it suddenly appeared out of nowhere. I have no idea where it came from or how far it extended. My anxiety increased with every step I took.

There it was. It was a fine, hazy mist that enveloped every fiber of my body. The feeling was one of a damp, cool spray that one can often feel whenever one ventures close to a waterfall. Still, the moisture was everywhere, making my body shiver from its coolness. It was a foggy type of wetness that, although it was unsettling, also had a quality that was somewhat soothing to the touch and my emotions.

I have no idea where I was. I had lost all sense of time. I had no sense of where I had even come from. I also had no sense of where I was going. There was nothing around me to indicate what was even happening to me. There was just this fine mist that was surrounding every fiber of my being. As I focused ahead of me, all I could see was this mist.

I continued walking. Soon, through this foggy moisture, I was able to make out a path that I was traversing. Right in front of me, I could see its outline. However, it would disappear in the foggy mist if I looked even a foot ahead of me. Turning around, I could only see the path that I was on right beneath my feet, as that path would also disappear in the mist the further I tried to look behind me.

Where was I coming from? Who was I? What was I doing here?

Most importantly: what was my destination? A multitude of questions entered my head. Despite the anxiety and apprehension, there was a sense of excitement as to what I would ultimately find. There was nothing in my journey to this point that would indicate that I was facing any type of danger.

I did remember that I had always been a man driven by faith. When times would be turbulent, my faith in God would deliver me from my darkest hours.

When times were good, God would also show me how to appreciate the events in my life. Any blessings I felt had been provided out of God's grace.

Now I found myself on this path, which seemed to have no beginning.

Looking ahead, it also appeared that it had no end. The more I continued to walk, the more I felt my legs begin to tire. My apprehension started growing more and more as I continued my journey.

After what seemed to be a limitless amount of time, I slowly started to make out the objects close to the path I traversed. First, my keen sense of hearing detected what sounded like a small bubbling creek next to the path. Looking over and squinting my eyes, I began to make out the ripples of the water that accompanied the sound. I also made out the outline of a few small wooden benches next to this sound.

Farther down the path, I thought I heard the sound of birds chirping in the distance. As the misty haze made it difficult to see, the sound became clearer the longer I kept wandering down the walkway.

Through a misty fog, a path, a small brook with benches, and hearing the sound of birds, I asked myself what else I would find on this unexpected adventure. I continued my trek. It was at that moment, I thought I heard a voice.

At first, it seemed almost undetectable. As I continued walking, the volume seemed to increase with every few steps I took. Finally, the sound was audible enough that I thought I could begin to make out what was being said.

It appeared to be a woman's voice. It had a soft, high-pitched tone clearly associated with a female. The words began to get clearer with every additional step. This voice appeared to be calling my name.

As I continued walking, I heard the voice appear to get closer. I looked around, but the mist inhibited my ability to see where I thought the sound had emanated. Something inside me yearned to discover where this sound was coming from. More importantly, I needed to know who it was that was calling me and how this voice knew who I was.

Moving forward, I was finally able to discern what appeared to be three bright lights on wooden poles in the distance. These lights appeared to be equidistant in a circle around something. This illumination was hazy but grew more distinct as I moved closer. As the glow grew clearer, I was able to make out the outline of what these lights sought to define. There was some sort of building beneath these lights.

Once I was within thirty feet of the structure, the mist seemed to evaporate. Along with the lights, there was a full moon right above the structure. There was a warmth in the air that I can say I never quite felt before. At that time, the structure became clearly recognizable. It was a white gazebo.

Around this gazebo, the mist was completely gone. This circular building was small and simplistic. The building was white and enclosed with white fencing. The roof appeared to have small triangular shingles with a grayish tone. Affixed to the top of the roof, there was a small white cross. Inside, there was a small circular oak table with two padded wooden chairs also painted white. Even though this structure seemed overly simplistic, there was a moving sensation to my being there at that time.

It was then that I made out the silhouette of a woman sitting by the table in one of the chairs. The woman appeared to be looking directly at me. I could see her lips begin to move. Once again, she uttered my name. With one of her hands, I could see her motion for me to come in and sit in the vacant chair.

There was no fear in my mind or heart as I approached. Rather, I was intrigued by this adventure and yearned to discover what exactly was happening. As I moved closer, my eyes met the eyes of this mysterious stranger, and we both smiled. At that moment, I sensed some surreal connection with this being.

I had many questions that I desired answered. Where was I? How did she know my name? What was she doing out in this place that seemed so secluded? Why did she appear to be alone? More importantly, I needed to know who she was.

She was a beautiful woman. It is most difficult to describe what I was seeing. She was dressed in a white satin evening gown with a pair of dark shoes with leather straps. These shoes were not exactly high heels, but neither were they completely flat. She wore no jewelry that I could see. Neither could I see any makeup; she seemed to be a natural beauty, merely as she was. She had a dark brown tint to her hair that was accentuated with a few curls in front and extended down toward the middle of her back. Her eyes were a gentle blue that seemed to radiate a sensitivity when she gazed at me. Finally, her lips had a soft fullness and warmth that attracted me to her in a most romantic way.

At that moment, she told me that she would answer all my questions in time. First, she told me that I needed to trust my faith. God would be bringing me significant changes in the future. She emphasized that God would provide the path that He wanted me to follow, just like the path that brought me to her. I would need to be conscious of the subtle indicators God would provide for me.

After she said this, she asked me if I would like to go for a very short walk.

How could I refuse the most beautiful woman I had ever seen?

At that moment, we emerged from the gazebo and began walking farther down the path opposite to the opposite direction that I had taken to arrive at the lights. In this direction, the mist had completely disappeared to be replaced by the clear crispness of the moonlight.

I saw with clarity the bubbling brook by the path. However, I could not see anything across the water except the misty fog that seemed to extend upward from the other side. I could also see vividly the wooden benches. These benches had a small design of a cross on the back.

Moreover, birds were actively singing in the air. Surprisingly, I could see that a few of these birds appeared to be doves. Their tone sounded like the most riveting orchestra composition. During this interlude, the woman did not say anything to me.

We continued walking and enjoying our serene surroundings.

Finally, she put her hand in mine. We sat down on one of the wooden benches sprinkled along the path by the water. She reiterated what she said earlier in the gazebo. She wanted me to be conscientious and pay attention to the signs God would provide. Yet she added one additional comment: God will ultimately bring you what you feel you lack and what you feel you have lacked all of your life. It just may take time and patience to get there.

I tried to obtain elaboration as to what she was saying. However, at that moment, I saw what appeared to be lightning in the distance. The singing of the birds disappeared. After that moment, this woman said nothing more to me. Only the sound of the bubbling brook permeated the air. A little while after this first sight of lightning, I heard what sounded like the loudest clap of thunder I had ever heard. I told the stranger we should leave and go to safety.

She agreed and understood. She released my hand and began walking toward a mist that was once again surrounding the path.

There was another streak of lightning. It was followed quickly by another very loud clap of thunder. I began walking briskly in the opposite direction from how I had gotten to the gazebo. More lightning ensued with quicker claps of thunder. I turned around. The strange woman was almost invisible when she also turned around and gazed at me. It was then that she said one last thing, "My name is Miri." One last clap of thunder and Miri was gone.

CHAPTER 2

Awakened to Today's Reality

Jennifer and the Law Office

As I opened my eyes from my slumber, I could see the time: 6:30 a.m. The lights from the alarm clock were flashing. There was also the obnoxious buzz of the alarm indicating it was time for me to get ready for a new day. Whereas I understood the reality, how could this be? The adventure concerning Miri appeared to be so real. Was it truly just a dream at its end?

My name is Frank Talcott. I am in my mid-thirties. I am a practicing attorney in a small town in northern Arkansas. I opened this office a mere two years prior. I handle any case that comes through my door. Additionally, I tend to the office responsibilities on my own. I did not yet have a significant clientele to enable me to invest in additional staff, like a secretary or receptionist. Still, with the trickle of business lately, I wondered how long I would have the finances to maintain this office.

Since the national economy had entered into a recession, finances became an important preoccupation in my life. How would I make ends meet? What would happen if I were forced to close this office? Would there be another means for me to endure in the event of a more significant hardship? These thoughts injected a significant amount of stress into my life.

However, my most important consideration was my wife. Her name is Jennifer. At first glance, Jennifer was an attractive Arkansas belle with a sweet disposition. She was a few years younger than me. She was also short and petite. She had short, dark brown hair with somewhat large, round, beady brown eyes that were friendly yet had a piercing quality when one gazed into them for any extended time. Superficially, she seemed to have a bubbly personality that naturally welcomes friendship with others. We seemed to be attracted to each other from the moment we met. I suppose it was this attraction that led to our marriage after an extremely brief romance. Unfortunately, what was masked underneath was a darkness in her personality that threatened our livelihood if not our very lives.

She had two children from a prior marriage. Her daughter was 9 years old and carried her name: Jenny. Her son Dalton was 7. They were very smart and well-behaved children. My only issue was my inexperience around children, as I never had children of my own. From the time we met, I was determined to make a life for Jennifer and her beautiful children.

As an attorney, I do a lot of thinking and analysis. I labored out of bed to begin this new day. I thought a lot about what had happened from the time Jennifer and I met until now. A few past events began to weigh heavily on my mind. The severity of these events led me to question the survivability of my marriage.

During my life, I had mainly been an introvert. I spent a lot of time reading and studying because I knew I wanted to be an attorney. As a result, I had never been popular with women. Since my parents died at a young age (their early fifties), early on, I needed someone to help fill the void of that loss. My parents and I had been extremely close.

My father had been a hard worker all his life. He worked for a manufacturing plant for over thirty years. He was a forklift driver at this plant. He had been healthy most of his life. However, one morning, he did not wake up. He died in his sleep. To date, there has been no understandable explanation about his passing. His death was very tough on my spirit. It made me question God and faith.

My mother's death was easier to understand. She was sickly as a child. This condition had affected a valve in her heart. Doctors speculated that she would eventually need surgery to replace this valve. Unfortunately, by the time surgery was imperative, she developed pneumonia and succumbed to this illness. In less than a year and a half, I had lost both my parents.

With Jennifer, I had a yearning to love and be loved. I had never experienced true love in my life. It was true that I had girlfriends in the past. However, these relationships were far from being classified as true love. My heart ached at the thought of living my life alone. My faith in God helped ease the ache of any loss. Jennifer offered the companionship I felt I needed.

The severe events mentioned created doubt that Jennifer was the true love I was supposed to be with. My overnight adventure cast more doubt with the very words Miri had uttered. She stated God would provide the signs and the path I need to travel. I remembered her saying that God would bring me what I lacked in my life. I needed to be patient and have faith. After I showered and got dressed, I began to wish that Miri was there to answer my questions and doubts as well as elaborate on why she even appeared.

I began to relive with a vivid clarity the adverse moments I have indicated. These events started immediately after our marriage. Our wedding was more of an elopement. We made a spur-of-the-moment decision that marriage was the right thing to do at that time. There was no hesitation to journey to get the license and find a qualified person to perform the ceremony.

We went a very short distance to the residence of a local justice of the peace. Jennifer had a good friend agree to be a witness. Unfortunately, because of the suddenness, I had no friends or family to appear as witnesses for me. Notwithstanding that issue, my main concern was to get married and begin my life with Jennifer and her children.

The ceremony was brief. After some introductory words by the directing official, both Jennifer and I exchanged handwritten vows concerning our love for each other. Afterwards, as in traditional weddings, we were pronounced married. Unfortunately, there was no time for a honeymoon trip. I still had to work to maintain a satisfactory standard of living for Jennifer and her two children.

When Jennifer and I first met, she worked as a van driver for a local health clinic. This position was short-lived when she was terminated after she had an acrimonious exchange with another van driver. While I did not understand what happened, as a man of faith, I was committed to respecting the marital vows I had taken. The fact that I was a struggling attorney with no other means of financial support continued to put added stress on our lives. Nevertheless, I began to open my eyes to the emerging thought that Jennifer had some kind of issues with her mental health. I prayed that God and faith would allow us to overcome our hardships.

Reality Affected by Jennifer's Mental Health

The instability of her mental health began emerging shortly after our marriage. Since I was an attorney, I had many professional as well as personal connections. Some connections were remote; however, a few were good friends with whom I desired to maintain contact. Moreover, some of these friends and acquaintances happened to be females. I incorporated these individuals into my email contacts on my computer.

This fact led to the first disastrous interaction between Jennifer and me. One day after a tedious day in the office, where I received a reprimand from a judge for words I used in court, Jennifer greeted me at the door. Her empty piercing eyes lacked any compassion. She wanted me to sit down so we could have an important, intimate discussion.

The intense discussion began when she stated she had received a phone call right before I arrived home. After answering the phone, a female on the other end asked for me. The caller stated that her name was Beverly, with no additional identifying information. Jennifer explained that I was in court but would arrive home later in the afternoon. As a result of this call, Jennifer began to demand that I eliminate all my email contacts. Moreover, she also conveyed the necessity for me to tell any other callers (female or male) not to call there again.

In the beginning, I tried to comfort Jennifer. I tried to explain that Beverly was merely the county public defender who was calling me on a legal matter. Specifically, she was calling to see how I was after hearing about the judge's reprimand. Beverly and I became professional colleagues immediately after I opened my law office. She was many years older, happily married with two children and a grandchild on the way. A platonic friendship was formed through our interactions.

Unfortunately, Jennifer did not want to hear this.

Jennifer was adamant that I delete all the contacts included on the computer. When I questioned her about specific reasons, she could not convey a succinct answer. She tried to articulate her uneasiness with my having female friends. While some of the contacts were individuals I befriended before I met Jennifer, I diligently tried to tell her that all the contacts were only utilized on a professional level. If she was insinuating these contacts were a basis for infidelity on my part, her fears were unwarranted.

During my career practicing law, I had an exemplary work ethic. This continued attitude was essential with our country's fiscal difficulties. Every morning, I awoke to the alarm, rose out of bed, showered and got dressed, and prepared to go to the office. During this quiet time, I frequently let Jennifer sleep. At times, she had spells of insomnia interfering with her rest. She even occasionally ingested medications like Benadryl to induce drowsiness. As our marriage progressed, she even had a therapist prescribe Xanax to alleviate her anxiety. I relied greatly on faith to see me through. Every morning when Jennifer was awake, I told her I loved her before exiting through the door.

When I arrived at the office, I made consistent attempts to stay in touch with Jennifer. I would either call or send texts to her. Moreover, unless my appearance in court was needed or if I had a special appointment with a client, I would always venture home to have lunch with her. With my faith and responsibility to my marital vows, I needed the comfort of knowing Jennifer was happy and in good spirits. I was as faithful and loving a husband as I could be. It was hard for me to realize Jennifer did not understand how I could even manage the time, even if I wanted to be unfaithful.

Mental health is a subject that people seem to attach a stigma. When someone has severe anxiety, the observer does not seem to understand. The common response is merely that the affected individual can get over it. For the afflicted person, this thought is easier said than done. At the time of this inaugural argument, even I did not quite understand the debilitating effects of Jennifer's anxiety.

While Jennifer continued to forcefully demand the elimination of the contacts, I likewise continued my resistance. This irrational bickering continued for some time. Our discussion finally reached a climax. It resulted in one of the most somber experiences I have ever had.

During my life, it is ironic to say that I hated to argue. I was an attorney whose professional job is to articulate points of contention. On a personal level, I am inclined to turn and walk out the door before emotions start to interfere with rational communication. Often, people, especially married couples, let emotions interject into the deliberation with adverse consequences. People say and do things that they ordinarily would have never fathomed.

This initial argument had continued far too long. I should have walked out to cool off before the boiling point was reached. After several hours, Jennifer and I had debated the subject of contacts on the computer. While I hated the thought of an argument ever becoming physical, the consistent arguing coupled with a lack of a meal was a definite precursor of what was to come. Our altercation eventually suffered physical overtones.

First, there was a little pushing and shoving in the kitchen. After a brief respite, we started our argument all over again. Our voices escalated in tone, yet it never occurred to me that a neighbor may have been listening to the sounds coming from our apartment. Soon, Jennifer sat at the end of our couch, right by the door. I was moving closer to the door to continue our word exchange.

In this position, it was then that I decided I needed out. My plan was to exit the door so I could rest, get a hold of my emotions, and let my irritation cool. However, that result did not happen. Jennifer held her arm in front of me to obstruct my passage. Instinctively and impulsively, I grabbed her arm and bit her hard close to her shoulder.

While every fiber of my being knew this was wrong, I believe the situation dictated the result and the ultimate end to this argument.

After this physical contact, Jennifer remained seated on the couch. I moved across the room to the loveseat diagonally opposite this couch. To say that I was not irritated and emotional was clearly an understatement. Jennifer seemed shocked at this turn of events and was trying to calm down, too. However, it was clear that the emotion of the night had only started. At that moment, our door, which had been opened a crack, slowly started to be pushed open. I heard a voice and saw what appeared to be a light coming around the corner. Eventually, the door was slowly pushed open more and more. It was then that I realized it was the city police department. The neighbor was concerned with events transpiring, so she needed to inform the authorities.

Upon identifying themselves, two officers entered the premises.

They asked both of us if everything was fine. I told one of the officers that we just had an argument. I also said that both Jennifer and I were starting to calm down. At that moment, the same officer asked the devastating question: Did the argument get physical?

All my life, I have learned the importance of telling the truth. Upon this inquiry, I told the officer that it did get somewhat physical. He asked if either one of us had hit the other or if there were any marks indicating domestic abuse. Not wanting to circumvent my faith and lie, I told the officer I bit Jennifer on the shoulder as I was trying to leave.

At that moment, my life completely changed. The inquiring officer stated he had follow-up questions while the second officer took Jennifer outside to question her. After discovering the bite mark, there was no doubt what would happen next. The officer questioning me placed me under arrest for domestic battery. He read my Miranda rights while placing me in handcuffs. I cannot convey how low my heart sank at that moment.

After some time, I was escorted to the police car and taken to the county jail. After being booked, I was placed in a holding cell awaiting the possibility that Jennifer would be able to bond me out. Other inmates were occupying a cell that had just one open toilet and one small lavatory. As I looked around and saw the other detainees in the large cell around me, I began to ask myself, "What have I done? What happened?" All I knew at that moment was that I had lost my freedom, which I valued so highly. Some semblance of that freedom would return a couple of hours later when Jennifer helped bail me out and took me home.

As I started the drive to the office, I thought that this altercation was the first sign that anxiety would be a troublesome issue for Jennifer and me. Our short marriage was riddled with issues like this first argument. However, they did not have the same intensity and shock as the email contact elimination issue had. Still, these additional episodes made it clear that our marriage may be incapable of being salvaged.

CHAPTER 3

The Need for a New Reality

Thoughts about Jennifer's Mental Health

*P*rior to arriving at the office, I decided to stop to purchase a doughnut and a small cup of coffee. I anticipated a light day. I would go a few blocks to the courthouse to finalize a couple of uncontested divorces. Afterwards, I had scheduled two other appointments: one to draft a will and the other to draft a land sales contract. My mind continued to be preoccupied with Miri and my turbulent marriage to Jennifer.

The email argument was merely one in a series where Jennifer's pronounced anxiety emerged to the fore. There was an incident after dining at a Mexican restaurant nearly a year ago. Almost six months later, her anxiety resurfaced during a trip to Dallas. Finally, two weeks ago, the climactic event that foretold our future occurred at the apartment. As I was sipping my coffee in the quiet confines of my office, I vividly relived each of those instances. It became clear that our marriage could not last.

The Incident at the Mexican Restaurant

When money permitted, Jennifer and I enjoyed eating dinner at local restaurants around town. Our favorite was one named Pablo's Mexican Villa. The ambience was soft and delightful. Furthermore, the food and service were incomparable. Finally, the setting allowed for fulfilling conversation.

On this occasion a year ago, Jennifer and I entered and waited to be seated. After a few minutes, an attractive hostess arrived to help direct us. She looked to be in her mid-20s to 30. She also appeared to be somewhat tall with straight sandy brown hair. She was dressed in a light orange-brown blouse with denim pants. We followed her to our table.

After being seated, Jennifer and I engaged in small talk. There was no indication that our excursion would be nothing less than an enjoyable evening out. We ordered, continued our amicable dialogue, ate, and then it was time to leave. Even as I approached the counter to pay, there was no way to predict what was to occur.

Upon arriving at the counter, I observed the cash register and a series of business cards next to it. There was something about the artwork on the cards that captured my attention. Out of the corner of my eye, I was able to discern the hostess crouching down to the left of the counter where I was standing. It was unclear exactly what she was doing. She was either cleaning or looking for something. Finally, she stood and greeted us again. I paid our bill and told her we appreciated the service. At that moment, we left.

After returning to our car, Jennifer's mood suddenly shifted. When we were in the restaurant, she was talkative and had a positive demeanor. However, in the car, she did not say a word. Her face seemed stressed, and any smiles were replaced with an almost ominous scowl. Something was wrong.

It was then that I made every attempt to get to the root of this mood change. Jennifer was reluctant to tell me. She assumed I knew what was wrong. I was left to guess. I told her I had absolutely no clue what was wrong. If I did something wrong, what it was remained a mystery to me.

I started the car to begin the short drive home. Almost immediately after pulling out of the restaurant, she stated that I had been gawking at the hostess. I expressed my astonishment at this insinuation. How was I gawking at the hostess? I tried to reassess all the facts: approaching the counter, staring directly at the business cards, observing the hostess with my peripheral vision, paying, and thanking the hostess. What did I do wrong?

Jennifer was adamant that I had been gawking at the hostess. I made it clear that if it appeared that way, it was not my intention. I was merely enjoying my wife's company, had been observing fine artwork on the business cards, and was anxious to get home to continue our delightful evening. The idea I had been staring at this hostess was a distant afterthought, if not an impossibility. She did not want to hear that. She thought she understood what she saw.

Upon arriving at our apartment, the conversation continued. She expressed her sentiment again. I counterpointed my interpretation. The bickering persisted until I had to excuse myself to use our bathroom. She stated that she would remain in the car. After a quick interlude, I returned to the car, but Jennifer was gone.

I began looking for her. While we had several neighboring apartments nearby, I slowly began a meticulous search to find her. I looked in and around our apartment to no avail. Afterwards, I began searching our driveway toward the driveways of neighboring apartments. As more time passed, I began to get extremely concerned.

After walking next to the driveway of another close, adjacent apartment, my eyes fixed on a slight grassy incline in front of its driveway. It was there that I could make out a silhouette of a person lying on his side. Only by walking closer did I realize that this person was a female. It was Jennifer.

I began my conversation by asking her if she was all right. She mumbled but was generally unresponsive. She also gave the impression that she was going to be sick. At that moment, a neighbor whom I had seen a few times before came by and asked if he could help. Thinking this situation was critical, I indicated that we needed to call 911. Still, I really did not know exactly what was happening.

The paramedics arrived and began treating Jennifer. Once her situation proved stable, she was transported to the local hospital. I was in shock at this turn of events. I needed to understand what had happened to her.

Once at the hospital, I was visited by the emergency physician. After asking additional questions, he stated that he had seen many cases like Jennifer's. Because of her anxiety at the restaurant, the events had created a very severe panic attack. While most panic attacks generally are short-lived and manageable, her brain was showing Jennifer the best coping mechanism for the thought she perceived at the restaurant. I was dumbfounded because I had never experienced anything like this in my life.

After being provided medication, Jennifer was discharged. We journeyed home, and nothing else was said about this episode. However, to date, her anxiety has created two detrimental episodes affecting our marriage. My guard rose since I had no idea if or when her anxiety would create problems in the future. At that moment, I began reviewing the files I would have in court that morning.

The Dealey Plaza Debacle

My heart ached as I recalled her first panic attack. I had never encountered anything of that magnitude in my life. I quickly went to court to finalize the two uncontested divorces. Upon returning to the office, I began to reminisce on the second episode. Tears began to form in my eyes as I recalled specific aspects of this encounter.

Throughout my life, I developed a keen interest in history. From the early days of the founding of our republic through the current time, I was fascinated by how historical events unfolded. My main interest focused on the period of the U.S. Civil War. However, Jennifer and I traveled to Dallas to experience a historical event firsthand: the assassination of President John F. Kennedy.

President Kennedy was shot in Dealey Plaza a few years after my birth. Conspiracy theories have emerged ever since that sad day in November of 1963. As I had never been there, I wanted to experience up close the location where this tragedy occurred.

When we arrived and parked, we walked down the sidewalk to the Texas School Book Depository. This building is a museum of the events of that fateful day. On the sixth floor, we saw the floor as it existed at that time. Moreover, we saw the stacks of boxes and the perch near the window where Lee Harvey Oswald supposedly fired the fatal shot. My main curiosity was to get a sense of whether Oswald acted alone.

After that initial enlightening tour, we departed the building. Walking down the street, we observed what has been called the grassy knoll. The grassy knoll is a small, sloping hill within the plaza. Toward the apex was a concrete wall. This area is off the street where Kennedy was shot. Conspiracy proponents have argued that a second gunman was present at or near this location or even hiding in the sewer under a manhole cover, where other shots allegedly were fired. The fascination with such an event is to formulate these various hypotheses.

Jennifer and I stood on the upper expanse of the grassy knoll for some time. There were others in that locale studying the scene as we were. Unfortunately, Jennifer did not seem to have the same enthusiasm. As we began to tire from the trip and the tour, we finally decided to leave.

As with the Mexican restaurant, Jennifer's tone abruptly shifted. I had no idea what was wrong. Upon questioning her, she gave no answer at first. Our conversation began with her stating that I should have known what was wrong. Once again, I believe that Jennifer thought I could read her mind.

Finally, Jennifer began to open up as to what was disturbing her. She claimed that there was a guy and a few girls down on the grassy knoll a little distance from the street. She was emphatic that I had been staring at those girls. I was dumbfounded again. There was little question that I was so engaged in the fascination of the locale we found ourselves that observing anything else was inconceivable. For me, it is impossible to be engaged in two things at once.

Upon leaving, like with the Mexican restaurant ordeal, our bickering was consistent. She wanted to believe what she saw. I also made the point that she was sadly mistaken. I made every effort to try to calm Jennifer down. At that moment, I was afraid that this event would escalate like the episode that led to my arrest. What I thought would turn into a most memorable outing turned into one I would rather forget because of its adversity.

The more I talked and denied her insinuations, the more Jennifer's emotions seemed to increase. As we were driving home and it was starting to get late in the afternoon, I stopped near Denton, Texas so we could get a room. There was no stopping Jennifer and her accusations. My main concern was the potential for the discussion to turn physical.

Once in the motel room, there began to be an eventual ebb to the discussion. Fortunately, the event never turned physical. It was clear that I needed to try to get help for Jennifer and me. Otherwise, more events such as those mentioned would prove fatal to our marriage.

I began to prepare for my afternoon appointments. The drafting of the will and the land sales contract would not take very long. Upon completion, I would think about how Jennifer and I did have one counseling session. Unfortunately, she and I never returned. Our problems appeared to quiet down. However, there was one last event that truly conveyed how detrimental Jennifer's mental insecurities would be to a lasting marriage.

The Climactic Trauma

While in my office, the tears inevitably began to flow. The third event had a crushing impact on my human psyche and spirit. As it happened only two weeks before, its events were still very fresh in my mind. I actually believe that I experienced some overwhelming and lasting trauma as a result.

That day two weeks ago began like any other. I got up, got dressed, woke Jennifer up briefly, told her I loved her, and departed for the office. During the day, I had a typical day with uncontested divorces along with appointments scattered throughout the afternoon.

Periodically, I sent texts to Jennifer to see how she was doing. Since her emotions had quieted as of late, she seemed very calm, and any insecurities vanished. Ever since the Dealey Plaza debacle, she had been taking an increased dose of Xanax to quell any emerging anxiety. However, all that would change once I arrived home. After a brief dinner and relaxation by listening to some quiet music, it was time for bed. It was then that Jennifer's conduct and words seemed to blindside me. She asked me if she was the most beautiful woman I had ever seen.

I was startled because she had never specifically asked me a question like that before. I initially hesitated, but eventually said that it was her. I emphasized that I was with her now and that was the only thing that mattered. It was this momentary hesitation that catalyzed the ensuing argument with her. She prodded me to give an answer as to why I hesitated.

I initially told her I could give no clear reason. I specified that my hesitation was that I had seen and dated girls when I was younger who were pretty. Additionally, I pointed out that the past was the past. I was with her now. It was these words that escalated into a serious argument between us.

She was unrelenting in her inquiry. She wanted me to clearly admit that she was the most beautiful woman I had ever seen. Anything less than a full-fledged honest admission would be unsatisfactory. Not wanting to hurt her feelings and not wanting to lie, I was at an impasse as to what to do and how to handle this event. I was very tired. I did not want to allow this situation to spiral out of control.

I hesitated again before telling her she was the most beautiful woman in the world. That was unacceptable to Jennifer. She let the bickering continue. No matter what I said or did, it remained unacceptable to her. The argument continued. I was rapidly approaching my boiling point. It was as if my head was in a vise and Jennifer was slowly turning it to cause me more and more pain.

The result was inevitable. I told her she needed to stop. She continued with her unrelenting verbal volley. Again, I told her the fight had to end. It was then that the argument turned physical.

My own mental state was beginning to be in question. I had had enough. I told her to be quiet or else. She continued. At that moment, I uncontrollably punched Jennifer in the stomach. While she was surprised, her bickering continued.

More punches. More bickering. At that moment, Jennifer asked for the phone. If I did not comply, she would scream. I relented momentarily, but finally capitulated to her demands. At that moment, I saw what appeared to be bruising on her stomach.

Similar to when I was arrested, my heart sank to its lowest abyss. I felt that I was in inescapable trouble. More importantly, I felt everything I had worked for was at stake. Specifically, this included my prize possession that I worked for all my life: my attorney's license.

When she took the phone, she dialed 911. At that moment, I went to our door and opened it waiting for the police to arrive. As she continued talking, I realized the imminent severity of what had happened. I would be arrested, lose my law license, and lose my marriage. My emotions were in ruins at that moment.

I waited and waited for the police to arrive. The only conclusion legally that the police could draw is that Jennifer had been physically abused. I would be arrested and left to face my demons. I thought to myself that Jennifer was the only person I had ever met that knew exactly what buttons to push to bring out the worst in me. My heart truly sank at this type of manipulation.

The police never arrived. Like a Hollywood script, Jennifer had feigned the 911 call. Why she did not actually call shows that she did have some sensitivity toward me and my welfare. Yet the trauma I experienced left severe scarring on my heart and in my mind. I knew then that Jennifer and I had to split.

While the tears began flowing like a stream, I needed to leave her. I needed to develop a strategy to reestablish my well-being. I did not yet have a plan.

However, with my faith and intelligence, I remembered the words Miri had spoken. I needed to follow the path that God provided and continue to reach for the faith needed to see me through this turbulent time.

CHAPTER 4

The Discovery of a New Reality

Leaving Jennifer

Life is a process of learning and maturing. It is a process where one learns by doing and experiencing.

Maturing involves making decisions and learning from those choices. It involves knowing what is right and wrong. Living healthy consists of making sense of what is positive for a person's health and well-being. Specifically, life involves understanding what is right for one's mental health as well as physical health.

My relationship with Jennifer was clearly a learning point concerning one's mental health. It was imperative that I began to understand its intricacies. Further, there were now at least four occasions where Jennifer's anxiety impacted my mental and physical security. Her explosive emotions also began to affect my livelihood.

While still at the office, I needed to make a quick assessment of what direction I needed to go. Not only did my livelihood appear at stake with the physical abuse I inflicted on someone I vowed to love and protect, but our very lives were in a risky volatile setting. I needed to discern the best way to learn and get beyond this mental health crisis.

It was at that moment I once again remembered Miri and her profound words. I also began to run bible verses through my head. The significant verse was found in Matthew:

Come to me, all who are weary and burdened, and I will give rest.
Matthew 11:28.

I began to pray and ask God to bless Jennifer in her battle with anxiety. Next, I prayed that God would provide me comfort during this tumultuous time. Finally, I concluded by asking God to direct me to the best path for me to travel.

Once again, tears started to form in my eyes. While I did not know exactly where I was going, I knew clearly that God would provide the path and the means to get there. I needed to reach deep to find faith and the understanding that God made certain promises. If I believed, He would secure the blessings that He felt I needed.

I was at a crossroads as to a crucial decision to make. Do I stay with Jennifer and confront her anxiety while seeking help, knowing of the risks of future problems? Or do I wash my hands of the problems and move down a different path God directs? Based on my marital vows, I needed to stay with Jennifer during good times and bad. However, I sincerely felt that God wanted me to take a different path. The last event had been nearly life-threatening for both of us. It was then that I decided that I would leave Jennifer.

Once this decision was made, I felt I needed to leave the area. I needed to make a complete break from Jennifer and the location. I knew I would be leaving the law. Even then, I felt it was the most prudent decision to make under the circumstances. My main concern with leaving would be how I would work and sustain myself.

Through God's word in the Holy Bible, He provides the means and the inspiration for us to get to where He wants us to go. Further, this path directs us to where we need to go. While I was always tense about change, I remembered another bible verse:

Seek the Kingdom of God above all else, and he will give you everything you need.
Luke 12:31.

With this inspiration, there would be little doubt that my faith in God would guide me, sustain me, and take me down the path to financial well-being.

Since I felt I needed a clean break, I felt I wanted to travel. Before leaving the office, I thought about possible employment that would allow me that luxury. It was then that the most obvious possibility entered my mind. I needed to be a trucker. Being a trucker carried significant security since there was always an overabundant need for professionals to take supplies cross-country,

Since the recession hit, Jennifer and I had little money saved. However, I felt that part of those funds could be utilized to cover the cost of attending a truck driver's training school. Upon completing the program (generally within a month), I would receive a commercial driver's license. Most importantly, I would have employment waiting for me with a major trucking company. I discovered that the nearest school was located a few hours away in North Little Rock.

I called this school and made plans to enroll. I submitted an electronic payment, and everything was set for my arrival. Ironically, the next class was scheduled on Monday, and today was Friday. I had little time to get ready to embark on this radical change in my life. I needed to pack. Most importantly, I needed to let Jennifer know of my intentions and that divorce seemed inevitable.

I did not know how Jennifer would take this news. Although her anxiety created difficult moments, she did have a degree of security with me working and providing for her. I also continued to care for Jennifer and her children. As I felt that I did not have the heart to tell her in person, I decided to write a lengthy note to her. This note conveyed my sorrow and sadness at having to leave. However, the circumstances created the necessity for the welfare of both of us.

Since my plan was in motion, I began the simple yet excruciating drive home. Tears had been flowing intermittently during this journey. Once at the apartment, I arrived at the door. I placed the note near the door handle and knocked. I returned to the car. I did not stop for my things, nor did I desire any interactions that might have led to a confrontation. I did not think Jennifer would understand. As I was pulling out, I saw Jennifer open the door and retrieve the note. Lastly, we made eye contact as I was driving away. I do not believe she had time to understand what was happening.

Later that evening, I arrived at the North Little Rock driving facility. I could see a few rigs parked in an enormous paved area with cones and markings. I approached the office, registered, and went to a small furnished room where I would begin my stay. My thoughts centered on Jennifer. However, it was more important that I continued having faith that God would provide the necessary path for me.

The Beginning of My New Adventure

I had always loved to travel. This desire began with the short family trips my parents would take to visit other family members. For example, we journeyed from Arkansas to eastern Tennessee to visit my maternal grandparents when I was young. As I was close to my grandparents, these periodic visits did wonders to maintain my faith and spirit. My grandparents would provide delightful home-cooked meals along with providing inspiration through bible verses and other pertinent quotes.

Unfortunately, my grandparents passed away a year before I married Jennifer. My grandfather died first from a lingering health condition. Shortly thereafter, my grandmother followed. I believe it was due to her heart being broken by the loss of grandpa. They were buried side by side in a small cemetery in eastern Tennessee close to the Kentucky border. While I miss them dearly, they helped instill my faith that God would provide the tools to be happy, healthy, and content in life.

I was enthusiastic about this effort during my first day at the school. While it provided a path for me, the undertaking also provided a distraction from my mental anguish caused by leaving Jennifer. My focus would help alleviate any residual trauma associated with the adverse moments with her.

During the mornings, classroom learning emphasized what information the student needed to be a successful trucker. In the afternoon, we would spend time in the trucks learning how to examine the safety of the truck. That was followed by learning basic skills such as shifting gears as well as operating a tractor-trailer in reverse. This learning had to be the most difficult because of the skill required. Not only did the driver have to consider the tractor, but he would also have to take the trailer into account in this effort.

After hours of engaging in this training, I slowly began to forget the pain that had brought me there. I focused on learning all the tools to become a safe and knowledgeable over-the-road trucker. Before long, I had reached the day of the licensing exam. While I was anxious, I had little problem in meeting the demands that were expected of me. I succeeded in obtaining my commercial driver's license.

At that point, I wanted to begin driving. Near Fayetteville, Arkansas, there were many different transport companies I could choose from. I soon had it narrowed down to three. They were Sunshine Logistics, Springdale Trucking, and Dale's Trucking Company. Because of the information I gleaned along with its name, I opted to join Sunshine Logistics Trucking Company. The potential for travel all across the country, but especially the South, attracted me to that opportunity.

I contacted Sunshine, and they greeted me with open arms. After filling out some paperwork, I was assigned to my own tractor. As an added benefit of being an employee, the assigned tractor was mine for as long as I continued being employed by Sunshine. Moreover, I could request that a part of my earnings be distributed for the ultimate purchase of this tractor. This arrangement made the truck available for both personal and other professional uses. This provision was especially helpful when a driver lacked his vehicle, as would develop in my situation. On the side of the semi was a drawing of the horizon with the sun and its rays slowly emerging from some clouds. It was an incredible sight.

Most importantly, it reminded me of one of the business cards I had seen in the past at the Mexican restaurant. Since I never believe in coincidences, there was a reason why that memory returned to my thoughts. Only God would provide the understanding as to the meaning of this connection.

After being provided with a new semi-tractor, I was assigned the location of my first run. I was to venture to Fort Smith, Arkansas, and transport a load to a location in Ontario, California. To prepare for this excursion, I went to a nearby Goodwill store to purchase some clothing. Afterwards, I traveled to a local retail outlet and got some other supplies, like a pillow, blankets, and other items for entertainment for this lengthy hiatus.

In the back of my mind, I thought about Miri. I thought about the dream. I had passing thoughts about Jennifer and how she was. Yet the overriding consideration was the feeling of a presence. I felt God was taking me by the hand and directing me somewhere that had a significant and inspirational purpose. Only by driving down that route would I be able to learn what this mission was. It was with that fleeting thought that I inspected the semi, started it up, and began a journey that would have far-reaching consequences.

CHAPTER 5

The Signs of Faith

The Old Woman at the Cross

My new adventure was beginning. I started driving toward a new future and a new reality. Memories of my old life with Jennifer were slowly disappearing. I had no idea where my life would direct me. Yet there was a calmness to my spirit since I left Jennifer.

While I was at the driving school, I received many calls and texts from Jennifer. I listened to every voicemail message she left. Further, I reviewed every text. As time progressed, the time between messages increased significantly.

A few weeks into my training, I composed a single text. This text merely stated that I had begun a new life traveling without her. I would pray for her happiness. However, I clearly dictated that a life together was not possible. Her anxiety cast a dark shadow over our hearts.

Immediately after sending that text, there was a quiet to her contacts. Sporadically, I still received messages. However, the quantity of the contacts diminished. When I was waiting to retrieve the loaded trailer in Fort Smith, I reviewed her last text. It said not to worry. Surprisingly, she mentioned that she had started seeing someone else. She would be in touch with me through an attorney.

That text cut my soul like a knife. Being conservative and old-fashioned, I had always believed that marriage was a lifelong commitment. However, with our four anxiety episodes and an attempt at counseling, preservation of our marriage would be an arduous uphill climb, if not impossible. Realizing the feeling I had done everything possible did little to quell the feeling that I found myself alone. The void created by the death of my parents seemed to rise from the ashes. The emerging sense was the need to love and be loved.

I refocused on the journey. I hooked up the trailer. Soon I would begin the long drive west. The trip would take a few days to complete. My thoughts returned toward the new adventure I was commencing.

The distance from Fort Smith to Ontario, California was close to 1500 miles. Since I had a few days to get the load to the destination, I planned to break down the trip in three equal segments. Each of these segments consisted of approximately 500 miles per day. It was sunny and warm when I managed to leave Fort Smith. I felt a deep sense of responsibility as I took the first turn and found myself on the interstate.

My first leg of the journey would be through Oklahoma. Eventually, I would leave Oklahoma and enter Texas below the Oklahoma panhandle. My first overnight stop would be near Amarillo, Texas. I was excited about what I might see along the way.

To my chagrin, the trip was relatively uneventful through Oklahoma. Other than a slowdown of traffic due to road construction near Oklahoma City, nothing out of the ordinary happened worthy of mention. However, that fact would change about 40 miles from Amarillo. I had an experience that made me question if it were actually real.

A traveler can see it from a significant distance on Interstate 40. There is a huge white cross beside the freeway. One will find this landmark around Groom, Texas. This cross is almost 19 stories high. That height equates to being approximately 190 feet tall. It was there that I decided to stop, park my rig, and stretch my legs. I was getting close to the stopping point of this initial part of my trek.

As I stopped and got some juice to drink in my cooler, a remarkable incident transpired. As I was looking in the direction of this cross, I began to have a vision. A figure had appeared underneath. As it caught my undivided attention, I had to take a closer look. As I approached, there was a form that appeared to be feminine.

I moved closer to investigate. I rubbed my eyes, and it was unclear whether it was real or not. This older woman was dressed in white with a white veil over her face. I was too far to adequately describe minute details of this encounter. Still, I seemed to detect a somber look emanating from her eyes.

I was so shocked and enthralled at what was happening that I dropped my juice on the ground. I was mentally noting everything I could comprehend about what was happening. She appeared to take her finger and point in the direction where I had come from. While she appeared to be saying something, I could not hear anything. After that gesture, the woman was gone. I started to wonder if what I had seen actually occurred. I had been driving all day, so I thought my brain was playing some kind of trick on me. Finally, as I got within an arm's length of the cross, I noticed fresh footprints in the sand by the cross. Oddly enough, I could see no one nearby who could have made those small prints.

As I was trying to digest this strange occurrence, I returned to the truck. I retrieved another juice and began to relax. I tried to convince myself the apparition was not real; I merely was seeing something I had fabricated in my mind. After finishing the juice, I started the truck and returned to the interstate.

About 40 minutes later, I arrived near Amarillo. It was there that I decided to relax for the evening. I set my alarm for 6:00 a.m. After I laid down to slumber, I continued dwelling on my past. I remained consumed by what I had seen. That event coupled with the dream with Miri about a month ago raced to the forefront of my mind. However, my main thought returned to that strange woman pointing east. What did that mean? Who was she? Soon I fell fast asleep.

The Captivating Sunrise

The alarm soon began that monotonous ring. It was time to start a new day. As I had been extremely tired, I did not remember any dreams. I was hopeful that a vision of Miri would reappear. I had so many questions I needed answered. Maybe I had been too tired to dream.

My morning plan was to shower, change clothes, and then eat before continuing the journey. As I was exiting the cab, I experienced another awe-inspiring event. I looked immediately to the southeast. I was captivated by an occurrence that left me speechless. At that time, the sun began its slow ascent. It produced an image worthy of photographic prestige.

I have always been amazed by how days start and end. Wherever I was, I enjoyed watching the sun rise and set. However, this sunrise had a quality I had never perceived. It was as if an elongated flame was coming up from the horizon. The light also appeared to have the shape of a figure. I even began to sense God's presence.

After staring at this sunrise, I began an intense analysis of the recent extraordinary occurrences. The appearance of Miri, the old lady at the cross, and now the incredible sunrise compelled my attention. What did all these signs mean? I felt that God had set in motion a plan and a path for me to travel. I had to discover the meaning of those signs. I maintained that thought as I prepared for the day.

I went into the store at the truck stop. I was able to shower, change, and get a few items for snacks and for my cooler. The time spent marveling at the sunrise placed my delivery behind schedule.

Nonetheless, there was no question the load would be delivered in a timely manner. I returned to the cab, started the truck, and returned to the interstate for another long day of driving. What other adventures would be in my path?

The Mysterious Couple

Reviewing the map, my next stopping point would be Holbrook, Arizona. The destination would be another 500 miles away. I would have plenty of time to think. I would be able to assess questions I needed answered if I ever saw Miri again. I continued to have no idea exactly where my life would take me. I only knew that by prayer and faith, God would ultimately guide and protect me.

My route took me across the border from Texas into New Mexico. Other than typical commercial vehicles traversing the countryside, the area seemed to be lacking other motorists. Maybe it was due to the warm and desolate area I found myself driving through. As I was starting to get lonely with no one to talk to, I turned on the radio to provide company and entertainment.

As my mind wandered, I began thinking of past loves I have had in my life. I thought about puppy loves present when I was younger, to the first love that I thought was true when I was attending law school.

These thoughts ended with the development of my relationship and eventual marriage to Jennifer.

I began to decipher that there were many meanings associated with potential love. I started to think that there was no real way to define what true love is. It is a sensation, a feeling that exists when two people realize that they can no longer live without the presence of the other. That feeling was far from what I encountered with Jennifer. That emotion seemed to be sympathy for what she was going through. It was a need to help her through her mental frailties. It was then that I thought to myself that I had never experienced true love in my life. Yet my heart was yearning to find that one special person I could never live without.

Eventually, I stopped to take an extended break at a truck stop in Albuquerque, New Mexico. It was at this truck stop that a mysterious couple approached my truck. This couple seemed to be in their mid-fifties. They seemed affectionate toward each other as they hugged each other and held hands as they approached.

I greeted them with the most affable of salutations. I asked if they had been married for a while. They smiled and asked if it were that obvious. I introduced myself. They gave their names; however, I could only get their last name: Jennings. After that formality, we made small talk for about 30 minutes. It was then that I asked them where they were going.

Unfortunately, the man stated that they had been in an accident sometime back. They were not injured as a sleepy driver veered into their lane, colliding with them. They had made it to the truck stop but had an important destination they had to get to as soon as possible. They were headed to a medical facility near Phoenix, Arizona. The woman asked if I could provide a lift.

After reviewing my route, I felt that it would not be out of my way to detour to Phoenix. I would merely take Interstate 10 to Ontario once I arrived there. However, I would have to sacrifice some rest to deliver my load on time. Not wanting to pry as to the personal nature of this journey, I told them it would be nice to have the couple to talk to. I told them to get in when we were ready to leave. Although this decision was against company protocol, I thought to myself that we both could use the company. They offered to pay a nice fee for the transportation, but I declined as I was heading in that direction anyway.

I planned to continue to Holbrook, Arizona. Once there, I would get a little rest and resume the journey. The mysterious couple told me that it was fine. They needed time to eat, make some important phone calls, and sleep a bit, too. Although this encounter seemed very cordial, I felt something deeper to this interaction than what I knew.

I was very tired upon arriving in Holbrook. At another truck stop, I showered quickly, ate, and returned to the cab. When I entered, the couple was sound asleep in each other's arms. I quietly relaxed in the driver's seat while I wondered what other developments would occur on this trip. It was up to me to interpret the significance of all these events.

After a brief nap, I awoke upon hearing the couple get something out of a bag they brought with them. They both had sandwiches with water. Upon seeing my eyes open, they apologized if they had disturbed me. I told them everything was fine as we had to get moving to get to Phoenix.

It was then that the man stated that his daughter's husband was in an oncology unit at University of Phoenix Medical Center.

The doctors were going to try a new treatment for him the next afternoon. All the family had been devastated to hear the news about his very malignant brain tumor. If this treatment was unsuccessful, the illness was terminal as there was nothing else the doctors could do.

It was heart-wrenching for me to hear about this young man. He was in his late 20s. He was too young to be going through an ordeal like this. I could only begin to feel sorrow for the man's daughter who must also be going through a very turbulent time. I expressed my sadness to this couple as we began the journey to Phoenix.

It would only take about three hours to arrive in Phoenix. I turned on the radio to some soft classical music. I was deep in my thoughts. I had another preoccupation with the couple and the man struggling for his life. My only thought and prayer was that the experimental procedure was a success.

Upon arriving in Phoenix, the couple provided explicit directions to the hospital. In the wee hours of the morning, I found this hospital.

After discovering the oncology wing, I dropped off this delightful, loving couple. I wished them well. I also told them my prayers were with their son-in-law. The man thanked me and said that God will continue to provide a path for me. He stated that I had to make sure that I found faith. God will bless me for my kindness and sensitivity. As I was departing, I wondered if I would ever see them again.

I pulled over at a rest area shortly thereafter. I used the restroom, freshened up, and dozed a little. I purchased some strong coffee from a vending machine to help wake me. Afterwards, I returned to the truck. After my whole ordeal, I would soon be arriving at the last stop to deliver my load.

The Voice, the Sign, and the Image

The extra catnap, along with the coffee, did wonders to recalibrate my senses. Soon, I started the truck to begin my last venture to California. Only a few miles remained until I would reach I-10 westbound toward Ontario. I began to feel excitement at what I was accomplishing. My first effort to drive a big rig was fraught with challenges along with adventure. There was no doubt that success would be the ultimate climax.

The main concern I had was the volume of traffic I would experience once I entered the metropolitan areas closer to the destination. I had heard horror stories from both driver trainees along with other Sunshine drivers carrying loads to this area. With the enormity of this challenge, I began to focus heavily on the task at hand. I could not afford any unnecessary distractions.

The traffic remained steady as I drove through the suburbs of Phoenix. From Phoenix to Tolleson to Avondale to Goodyear, the traffic was moderate but very manageable. Nothing out of the ordinary inhibited my journey. It continued to be sunny and warm. I turned on the radio to listen again to the classical station to provide company on this last leg.

As I continued, traffic thinned out considerably. The vivid landscape served as a reminder of my location. I was driving through desert with cacti along with a few hills in the distance. It was sandy and dry. For a moment, I decided to roll my window down briefly. It was then that I thought I heard a voice calling me.

The sound took me completely by surprise. I even turned the radio off with the hope that I could hear the sound again. In the midst of the quiet, I did hear the faint sound of something. However, I could not make it out. It sounded like a female voice uttering my name. While it was so brief, eventually I did not hear anything else but the sound of the wind entering my window.

As I rolled the window up, I continued driving. Since there were few vehicles around me, I was able to focus again on the dry, barren landscape. While the music on the radio helped comfort me, pangs of loneliness once again made their presence felt. It was obvious that I would need to find some kind of company to quell that sensation. The anxiety had been creeping up in me almost to an excruciating level. Yet I remembered what Mr. Jennings had said. He said to make sure I found faith. I began to say a few prayers.

I was making excellent time as I continued my trip. Closer to California, I began to experience dry intermittent rolling hills.

Periodically, there would be brief areas of road construction. However, it was as if the land was telling me I would be leaving Arizona. I eventually reached an agricultural inspection station. At that moment, I crossed over into California.

Once near Blythe, I decided to stop to take a quick break. I was relieved that I had made it that far. As I ate a sandwich and drank another juice, my thoughts returned to the strange events that had occurred since Miri's dream. I thought that once I started the return trip home, the explanation would be provided for me. I remembered the more pertinent words Miri said. I needed to be patient.

As I drove closer to my destination, I rolled my window down again. Since the traffic was sparse, I listened carefully for any extraordinary sounds. I could only hear the sounds of my truck traversing in the wind. Additionally, there was the hum of other vehicles passing me. While I felt empty, I knew from past experience that other remarkable events would occur in the future. I was learning patience.

Closer to Ontario, the landscape began to be a bit hillier, along with a few curves. I knew it was only a matter of time before I arrived in a more metropolitan area. While I remained anxious, I was excited the closer I drove to the objective. All my thoughts focused on driving safely to the endpoint.

Soon, the metropolitan suburbs were upon me. I reached the outskirts of Indio, California. I took another brief break to refresh myself. My destination was only 90 minutes away. During this brief interlude, my thoughts again focused on Mr. and Mrs. Jennings' son-in-law. I never had the occasion in my life to experience a bout with cancer, but meeting and getting to know this couple warmed my heart in a way that it never was before. Would I ever see or talk to this pair again?

Continuing my drive, I was amazed by the small mountainous terrain in that locale. Present there were the Santa Rosa and San

Jacinto Mountains. I began to see why this area was popular with tourists. As I had no time to sightsee, I was hopeful that maybe one day in the future I could return to this area.

Traffic began to pick up significantly as I drove beyond Indio. From Bermuda Dunes to Palm Springs, it was tolerable, yet it began producing significant stress. All my attention was focused on driving. I was not as concerned about myself. In all manners, I was a defensive driver. I was worried about the others who were streaking around me. At that moment, I prayed that God would provide safety and security for the rest of the excursion.

With an hour left on this trek, I was near Palm Springs. At that moment, I glanced over quickly and saw a billboard that caught my eye. Fortunately, I was able to quickly discern what it said: "Faith will provide your answers." What did this mean, and why did I see that sign at that moment?

From Palm Springs to Loma Linda, traffic started to be a bear. While the pace was steady, any driver had to be alert to everything that was occurring around them. Cars were crossing in and out of traffic.

Additionally, they were zooming around me. Yet I was so close now. Soon, I would be in Ontario.

I arrived in Ontario later that afternoon. I managed to find the destination and deliver my first load. I was greatly relieved at the end of this trek. It would take some time to process this load. Subsequently, I would try to find a place to rest for the evening.

I noticed a sign for a truck stop as I waited for my delivery to be unloaded. The delivery consisted of parts in boxes that needed to be shipped to the area auto parts stores. I felt a sense of accomplishment when I completed this journey. However, the stress weighed heavily, and I felt worn out.

After the load was processed, I ventured to the advertised truck stop. It was an enormous facility for many rigs to park. I decided that I would journey to the rear of the truck stop so I would not be around many other vehicles. I would be close enough to utilize the facilities.

After showering again and having a decent meal at a restaurant inside, I returned to the confines of my truck. I had a battery-powered CD player where I inserted a Christian music composition. This CD had many modern faith-based songs. It surely was a welcome relief after the long day I had. Now I would wait until Sunshine gave me instructions for the next load after directly depositing my recent earnings into my bank account.

After a brief doze, I awoke to see that the lot was very dark. However, I could see people walking around the various semi-trucks. These individuals were scantily dressed. There could be no question that they were women. I had heard a lot about these people from other drivers I encountered in school and during this latest trip. These individuals had their own unique name: lot lizards, or prostitutes known for their work at truck stops.

After my initial observation, I eventually heard a knock on my passenger side window. There was a girl dressed in skimpy attire who could be no more than in her early twenties if not younger. She had multi-colored hair with a few tattoos on both arms. I rolled down the window. She asked if I desired some company for the evening. She called herself Crystal.

I was in shock. However, my shock soon disappeared in favor of rational thought. I had been lonely since my split with Jennifer. I also had been lonely for most of the trip to Ontario. I can say that I was tempted by this young lady's offer. Yet, at that moment, another extraordinary event happened.

Looking at a hill over Crystal's right shoulder, I saw an image. Like the image at the cross, it was a younger woman with a look of concern on her face. She almost had the appearance of Miri. At that distance, I could not really tell. She appeared to be voicing one word directed to me: NO! At that moment, it was clear what I needed to do.

I respectfully declined Crystal's offer. I wished her well as she ventured off in the direction of other trucks. Before her departure, I told her I would pray for her. My faith was working toward great things with me. I felt that if she had faith, God would help guide her, too.

What a journey I had on this trip! The old lady at the cross, the sunrise, the mysterious couple, the voice in the wind, the billboard, and now another female image occupied my mind. What was happening to me? Was I just tired from the drive and the stress? Was I lonely from my marital separation? As I pondered each of these questions, I slipped off into a very deep sleep.

CHAPTER 6

The Apparition Returns in the Mist

Direction from Miri Continues

The heavy mist once again consumed my body. I did not recall that the mist had ever been so heavy. There was also a gentle breeze blowing from my back. It was as if the wind was prodding me to an indeterminate destination.

Shortly, I rediscovered the path that I took to eventually observe the apparition in the mist. Now I know that her name was Miri. Who was she? Where did she come from? Why did our paths cross? Maybe during this interlude, I would finally receive the answers that my heart craved.

Realizing I had control of my faculties, I had many other pertinent inquiries. I felt Miri would have those answers as well. Who was the old woman at the cross? Why did she possess a somber look? Why did she point east? Moreover, why the captivating sunrise? Why did the sound of the voice in the wind beckon me? Why was the message of faith on the billboard that caught my eye at that particular time? Finally, why the image during the dialogue between Crystal and me? I could only acquire peace in my mind through these answers.

As the stiff wind kept pushing at my back, I continued walking forward. At that moment, I saw a flash of light in the distance through the mist. The faint sound of thunder reverberated in the air following the initial flash. As more flashes occurred in shorter succession with even louder thunder, I sensed this journey would be short.

Traversing this path, I was mesmerized upon hearing the sound of the small brook on my right. Next, I heard the birds begin to playfully chirp in the distance. Then the three lights appeared above the gazebo. At that point, I heard the soft sound of a recognizable female voice.

Approaching the gazebo, I could see the figure making the sound. It was Miri. Inside the building in front of a tall cross, she was on her knees with her hands clasped together. She appeared to be praying.

During this encounter, she was wearing a dark gown with a black veil. I sensed something might be wrong.

After a few minutes, she glanced over at me. Our eyes met. At this contact, she appeared to smile. She greeted me by name. I also returned the sentiment by calling out her name, Miri.

When I got closer, I extended my hands. She stood and extended both of her hands toward me. Upon clasping our hands together, she rose while asking me if I wanted to walk again. I nodded with a smile. I also commented that I had so many unanswered questions. However, seeing the lightning and hearing the intermittent thunder, I acknowledged that this rendezvous would only provide a cursory moment.

We arrived at the bench where we had our first quiet conversation. The cross on the back had an illumination I do not remember seeing during our first meeting. Yet the brook and the birds were just as I remembered. I was anxious and excited at the prospect of finally receiving answers to the questions that had provided periods of consternation.

I began by asking who she was and where she came from. I also expressed an urgent desire to understand what she had said to me in our prior fleeting encounter. Where was my faith taking me? When would I receive the answers that I so ardently required? What was the meaning of the signs I had experienced when I was driving? Would she know or have the answers? I stared at her beauty as I awaited an explanation.

After a brief pause, she started by saying the immediate future would provide the answers. She said she was proud of the path my life was taking. Like a jigsaw puzzle, the pieces would come together and create the solution I was looking for. She appeared to provide an illusory answer. Finally, she added that prior contacts would assist in revealing the knowledge I needed. By traveling east, I would have the ultimate solution to all my inquiries.

Taken aback by her reply, I recommitted to asking my questions. I was hoping she would give a more succinct and direct explanation. The next words she uttered were to chastise me over the need for patience.

She stated that this feeling is most important at this time in my life. Moreover, she articulated that events and understandings happen in God's time, not ours. I felt like a little boy who had been reprimanded for sneaking his hand into a hidden cookie jar.

Yet she did have a few more bits of wise dialogue that helped temper my anxiety and pain. She mentioned that family had been vitally important to her. Occurrences in her life had separated her from the most important individuals she remembered. While she was unsure why she was there, her presence was needed to convey to me that by assisting me, she would be providing an essential link with her family.

By traveling east, more events in my future would raise levels of inquiry as to what was happening and what would occur. There would be people I would interact with that would provide hope as to the validity of my life's direction. She expressed her hope that one day we would meet again. At that moment of contact, I would understand the entire picture being painted on a blank canvas.

My mind was a jumble as to events transpiring. Since I noticed a darkness about Miri, I asked her why she seemed somber and appeared to be praying. Her response was remarkably enlightening. She simply mentioned that someone from her life was about to experience another tragedy. Feeling that this person would lack essential comfort from others around her, she boldly mentioned that her heart ached for her loneliness. At that moment, a tear started trickling down her cheek.

Before I could solicit further elaboration, the wind had suddenly changed direction. It was moving from the opposite direction. At that moment, I told Miri we had to go. We rose from the bench and let go of our hands. She headed toward the path in the opposite direction from the gazebo. After a few moments, she turned around and said for me to look for faith. That effort would provide the needed answers. After these words, a solid fog appeared around me. Seconds later, everything was dark.

Miri Directing me East

My eyes popped open at the sound next to me. It was the annoying sound of my phone ringing. Through a text message, Sunshine Logistics was notifying me of my way deposit. More importantly, this text notified me of my next load route. I would need to travel to Knoxville, Tennessee. Upon picking up a load of retail art supplies, I would need to deliver this load to Oklahoma City to be distributed nationally. Was this the trip east that Miri was referring to?

I would have several days to travel to Knoxville. I committed to relax and enjoy the ride. I also made personal plans before picking up the load. Since it would be in the direction I was heading, I decided to place flowers on my grandparents' graves. I had not been there for a while. It would be refreshing and soothing for me to pay this area a quick visit. Finally, I took heed of the directive of Miri that I head east.

I had many chores to complete before undertaking this next trip. I had to do laundry. I had to get more supplies. I needed to stock my cooler. Finally, I needed to contact Jennifer to see how she was and how the divorce was progressing. Naturally, I would need to be sent or served papers while in my truck. I had no stable home at the moment. I would have plenty of time to think about life, patience, faith, and the path my life was taking. While apprehensive, I felt my journey was only going to get better.

It was after 10:00 a.m. With the eastern time difference, I did not have as much time to prepare as I originally estimated. However, laundry would be a short task as well as shopping. I would even have a little time to rest. Notwithstanding these chores, I planned to head out very early the next morning.

After doing laundry, getting supplies, and eating, I managed to rest a little. I relaxed to the sound of the Christian music I had played the evening before. During my rest, I was distracted by the ringing of my phone. My friends and professional colleagues knew I had been driving, so they were aware that my time was occupied. It was then that I realized this call could be from only one source.

After I dropped off Mr. and Mrs. Jennings at the Phoenix hospital, I insisted that they keep me informed of the status of the health of their son-in-law. Graciously, we exchanged telephone numbers. Once they knew something about the effectiveness of the experimental treatment, they stated they would contact me immediately. This couple was calling to provide this information.

Upon answering the call, I detected emotion in the sound of Mrs. Jennings's voice. I told her that it was good to hear from her, to stay calm, and to tell me what was happening. At that moment, she was sobbing and could no longer speak. I then heard Mr. Jennings's voice on the phone.

Whereas he had a kind greeting, he told me he had to convey some bad news. Almost in tears, he explicitly stated what had transpired after my leaving the hospital. In brief, they tried the experimental treatment with little success. Their daughter had arrived first at the hospital to look after their son-in-law. She had conveyed the bad news to him and Sarah. All four had returned home after the hospital furnished plane tickets. Now there was nothing to do but wait.

I was deeply saddened by this news. I wanted him to keep me apprised of his son-in-law's condition. I also wanted to know where Mr. and Mrs. Jennings lived so I could send correspondence, a card, or even flowers, if necessary.

Surprisingly, he mentioned the location: just outside of Nashville, Tennessee. Finally, I asked him the name of his son-in-law. He quickly replied, Gabe. I told him to have faith, as I would continue to pray for a miracle. I could sense tears running down his cheeks.

Before ending the call, I told him I would be traveling in that direction. Although I had little time to stop to visit along my route, I told him I was hopeful that I would visit on my return trip toward Oklahoma City. He manifested his appreciation. He was grateful for all I had said and done. He mentioned that his name was Charles. His wife's name was Sarah. He said that they were full of warmth to have a friend like me. After those words, we hung up.

Before lying down for my evening slumber, my mind once again returned to Gabe. I had experienced tragedy with my parents. I could not begin to fathom what it was like to lose a child, even an in-law like Gabe. My deep sentiment was also directed toward Charles's and Sarah's daughter. There was a sense of unfairness associated with this matter. I prayed to God why good people have to suffer bad tidings in an already cruel and uncertain world. God would provide His answers in His time. Finally, the old woman at the cross and Miri's words rumbled like thunder in my mind: go east. Upon that thought and the playing of Amazing Grace, I again drifted off to slumber.

CHAPTER 7

At Last, the Road to Faith

The Return of the Old Woman at the Cross

As darkness continued to blanket my rig, I awoke to continue driving down the road of my new adventure. My mind focused on the trip east. Additional thoughts revolved around what Miri had said. My heart was also preoccupied with Mr. and Mrs. Jennings. Would Gabe experience a miracle? What lasting effect would his illness have on this family? While a part of me was anxious, I was excited to follow the path God was revealing to me.

Since this journey to Knoxville and Oklahoma City would take several days, I planned to break it down into nearly equal segments. Like the itinerary to Ontario, I would spend the first night at a truck stop in Holbrook, Arizona. I would spend the following night near Amarillo. Finally, I would arrive in Little Rock on the third evening. I was hopeful to let Jennifer know about this plan. Any divorce papers could be served or even signed at that time.

I experienced nothing out of the ordinary along the way to Amarillo. Other than a few torrential downpours after entering Texas, the driving was almost boring. Traffic was light apart from urban areas.

Even in those areas, the driving was very tolerable. It was during the morning of the third day that I experienced another extraordinary occurrence. I had decided to revisit the cross near Groom, Texas.

Once at the cross, I decided to rest and eat a snack. After a few minutes of eating and contemplating life, I glanced at the cross. Another faint image had appeared through the glare of the sun's rays. I rubbed and squinted my eyes. The image became progressively clearer with time. I noticed another trucker who had pulled in the space next to me.

He was also staring at the image. No longer did I feel I was imagining this vision.

The image was of the same older woman I had seen before. She bore a striking resemblance to Miri, only she appeared older. She wore a darker outfit. Her attire reminded me of the dark gown Miri was wearing during my last visit to the mist. My first thought centered on the feeling that something was wrong. Was she also connected in some way to the individual whom Miri mentioned who would experience a tragedy?

As the image grew closer and crisper, the old woman made a gesture toward me. I was startled by this movement. She smiled and reached out to me with both hands. It was as if she beckoned me for a hug. The trucker to my left appeared as shocked as I was.

Sadly, just as quickly as the image had appeared, she vanished. The other trucker asked me if I knew what happened. I could only say that I was walking down a path to my future. God was directing me through vividly indistinct events. My comprehension of these events was elusive. Patience would reveal their meaning in time.

Upon examining the area around the cross, we discovered freshly made footprints. Again, there was no indication of anyone around who could have made them. The other trucker merely shrugged his shoulders. My only thought was that someone I had met or someone I would meet would have a connection to this vision. Could Mr. and Mrs. Jennings have an integral bond with these voices and images I had experienced, including Miri?

Jennifer, the Divorce, and Mental Illness

I started my truck and resumed my journey. While I was dwelling on this image, my thoughts began to turn to Jennifer. My next destination was Little Rock. Before leaving the cross, Jennifer had sent a brief text. She was responding to a text I sent the prior morning. My text informed her about my trip to the area. It also inquired as to the status of a divorce. Jennifer's response conveyed that she would arrive in Little Rock before dusk. She would bring divorce papers for me to sign. With my parents gone, there was a growing sense of emptiness developing inside my heart since I would no longer have a companion in my life.

As I drove through Oklahoma, a cool, steady rain beat down on my truck. Traffic was still light and manageable. I tried to comprehend the reality of my circumstances. Remembering Miri's words, it was imperative that I remain calm and patient. In time, all my life experiences would merge together into a majestic masterpiece rivaling any work of past renowned artists.

Several hours later, I entered Little Rock. Jennifer and I had predetermined where we would rendezvous. To make it easier for her, I took the bypass to North Little Rock. There was a truck stop close to the driving school. I would sign the papers there, provide the keys to the car since Jennifer may need it more than I with her children, and then proceed on my way. Nothing would be contested. I truly wanted to avoid any possible confrontation. I was sad enough by the circumstances. Any tension would be detrimental for both of us.

When I arrived, Jennifer was already there. Notably, she was not alone. After formal salutations, she introduced me to her new boyfriend. She expressed a somewhat urgent need for both of us to sign the papers. She wanted to return home to begin a new life.

As I was signing, I briefly tried to delve into her mind. I asked her a few questions. Why was she so anxious about me? Was it her love and jealousy toward me? Did she view any female anywhere as a threat to her? Finally, did she have her own sense of inadequacy? She remarked that she did not have a firm answer. It could be a combination of all those factors contributing to her anxiety and mental health. Her uncertain responses did little to quell my anxiety and concern about not knowing the true answers to all the questions I was pondering.

We were there briefly. Like the blink of an eye, we signed the papers, and we were traveling our separate ways. Sadness enshrouded my heart. It was as if storm clouds surrounded me after a once pleasant day. At that moment, I was without the true love I thought I had. Still, the circumstances warranted the necessity of our parting. At that moment, my main prayer to God was whether I would find that true love I so yearned for. Would I find that one special someone I could not stand to be without? Only time and faith would tell.

I originally thought I would spend the night in Little Rock. However, with the flashbacks to the past trauma of my life with Jennifer, I felt it imprudent to stay. Memories of the anxiety episodes would consistently permeate my thoughts. I would have difficulty resting and concentrating. With the long journey ahead, I needed to remain strong and focused.

I began to realize the value of strong mental health. Mental health conditions did not seem to be treated with the respect I felt they needed. Again, my thoughts digressed to the attitude many people possessed that a person with a mental illness could just get over their problem. Explain that idea to those like Jennifer who even have trouble understanding anxiety. It was not that simplistic. In some fashion, I thought to myself that I needed to become an advocate for mental health.

Introduction to Faith Elizabeth Jennings

I started down the interstate toward Memphis. I only had a couple of hours before I arrived. At that point, I planned to relax. I always enjoyed trips to that area. I wanted to park my rig by the mighty Mississippi River. I just wanted to unwind and sense its tranquil enormity. For its size, it had a serenity uncharacteristic of a massive entity. I wanted to walk, think, digest, and contemplate my life. My focus would be on faith and what God has in His plan for me.

The rain I had experienced in Texas and Oklahoma had ended. The temperature had moderated. It was very pleasant during my ride out of Little Rock. I once again played the Christian music that had been so soothing since I began my new trucking career. I renewed my thoughts about Miri, Charles and Sarah Jennings, and their son-in-law, Gabe. I needed to call Charles and inquire how the family was coping.

At that moment, I saw a shooting star dart from the clear Southern delta sky. Although it was for a fleeting moment, the light was vivid while it existed. Since I was a boy, I have rarely had the opportunity to see such a unique phenomenon. Amazingly, moments later, I saw another one ahead of me. This second falling star was dimmer than the first. I was shocked to see one. In a short time, I had seen two. What did this mean? Another sign from God? I was hopeful that my faith would convey the answers.

Moments later, I saw the beautiful skyline of Memphis, Tennessee. I saw lights from the bridges greeting drivers to this historic location. I was tired from the events of the day. I just wanted to pull over, stretch my legs, and relax from another interesting ride. I crossed the bridge into Memphis and pulled off on a side road by the Mississippi River. I found a place to park, shut my engine off, said a brief prayer, and began a short walk. I would never have imagined my life would forever change in the next few minutes.

The reflections of the lights of the city permeated the darkness toward the river. The Mississippi River was quiet with little traffic or noise. It appeared to be resting from a trying day. I could only see one small barge in the distance with a tiny tugboat guiding it. I was alone in the emptiness and solitude of my own thoughts. This peace was soon interrupted.

My phone started ringing in my pocket. I answered the call from a familiar voice. It was Charles. His voice seemed subdued as if trying to refrain from showing emotion. I greeted him and asked him how he and Sarah were. He simply stated that he had some very bad news. I knew at that moment the information centered around Gabe. However, I discovered his sorrow did not end there.

With his voicing starting to shake, Charles tearfully said that Gabe had died about thirty minutes before he called. All attempts to prolong his life were to no avail. The cancer was such an indiscriminate scourge. It had progressed so rapidly that it took the air out of the family's distraught lungs. It seemed as though they just had time to say a prayer for him. Then Gabe was gone.

At that moment, I felt an enormous sadness come over me. As tears started to form in my eyes, I remembered the shooting star I had seen during my ride to Memphis. I saw it about the same time Charles indicated Gabe left this world. Was this simply a coincidence or a sign from God? Not believing in coincidences, I firmly believe God was conveying important signs ever since Miri first appeared. I would need to adopt a method to understand the meaning of occurrences like these.

I expressed my sorrow to Charles. I spoke briefly to Sarah. With tears flowing from both of us, I made it clear that I expressed my sympathy and that I would try to do anything in my power to comfort them during this tragic time. I was still planning to stop in Nashville after picking up my load on my way to Oklahoma City. Sarah could not speak anymore, so she put Charles on the phone.

While I sensed Charles felt comfort in my words, he told me of another concern he had. It was his daughter. She had experienced tragedies since her birth. She seemed to be subdued by a prevalent depression affecting every aspect of her life. This depression grew more significant after Gabe had first been diagnosed with the tumor a year ago. He thought the worst upon her learning of Gabe's swift passing.

I do not recall the exact length of time I conversed with Mr. Jennings about his daughter. It was as if he gave me her life story, hoping I would be a miraculous angel to enter all of their lives and make them better.

The story began with a tragedy surrounding her birth, her trying childhood, her struggles merely to survive, her first meeting Gabe, a miscarriage, another baby dying at an early age because of cancer, and finally Gabe's recent passing. My heart wept at hearing the trying life this faithful woman had endured. I wanted to hold her and tell her everything would be fine. God would take both of us to where He wanted us to go. All my thoughts now centered around her. As an attorney, I tried to be a problem solver. I wanted to fix her life to help her escape her depression. Yet I did not know the power God would have in our ultimate interactions. Surprisingly, her name was Faith Elizabeth Jennings.

CHAPTER 8

Faith Elizabeth Jennings

After a restless night in the cab of my truck, I got ready to begin a new day early the next morning. I cannot recall how long Charles and I talked. However, I would have to guess it may have been an hour or two. It was during that conversation that I felt I had known Faith Elizabeth Jennings, all my life. In the back of my mind, I knew I had to make the effort to console this young woman by meeting her in the future. After I completed my morning routine, I felt refreshed to begin driving again. I showered, got dressed, and ate a sausage muffin from a local fast-food outlet at a truck stop. I had to concentrate on the job at hand. The destination of Nashville was only a couple of hours away. It was there that I planned a rest stop. Moreover, I developed an agenda upon my arrival. I would need to get the flowers for my grandparents' grave. I would also require a few more supplies for the continuation of this lengthy excursion. Afterwards, I would need to eat. I had the time and the hunger to sit for a modest home-cooked meal. After no more than a couple of hours, I needed to stay on schedule. I had to be in Knoxville the following morning to pick up the required load.

During my drive to Nashville, I thought of every aspect of the life of Faith Elizabeth Jennings that Charles conveyed to me. These thoughts made me feel I was watching a home movie Charles had prepared for me. For some reason, I felt an invisible connection to this young woman. Knowing every fact about her life fueled my desire to know and understand more of her thoughts and feelings. I realized a sense of emptiness she would possess after the death of Gabe. I had experienced loss with the death of my parents. I did not yet comprehend the extent of the emotion Faith would feel with all the tragic losses in her life.

The weather was tolerable yet foggy upon the drive out of Memphis.

Faith's childhood gradually entered my thoughts. She was born in Nashville and had lived in the vicinity every year of her short thirty-year life. Unfortunately, after her birth as a maternal twin, the other baby developed a respiratory ailment and did not survive. She had always told her father that she possessed an unusual connection to this twin.

That was just the beginning of a pattern of heartache for Faith. Her parents (Charles and Sarah) were hard workers all their lives. As a result, they did not have much time to spend properly rearing their family. Their focus was to keep food on the table and a roof over their heads. Although Charles and Sarah did not say it, I believe they were also deeply affected by the loss of the twin. However, they loved Faith with all of their hearts and appreciated her presence.

Charles originally came from South Central Kentucky. He had been a blue-collar worker all of his life. His working career originated as a coal miner. Realizing the dangers associated with this vocation, he decided to relocate to Nashville. A new auto parts plant had opened. It was at this plant assembling parts that he got his start in manufacturing. He worked his way slowly up the plant hierarchy. After twenty years, he was ultimately promoted to the position of Production Supervisor. This position required a lot of time and energy. This advancement was remarkable considering the most education Charles completed was a few vocational courses after a few years with this company.

Sarah, on the other hand, was from the Nashville area. Although she had a cute demeanor in school, she was frequently picked on by her peers. While she had a great deal of common sense, she did not have the patience or temperament to pursue an education after high school. Her main love was the love of flowers. She had dreamed one day of opening her own flower shop.

To help her financially in this pursuit of her own business, she became a waitress at a local restaurant. This restaurant served popular homemade dishes. However, this restaurant never really grew. Fortunately, the clientele was sufficient with accompanying tips to provide just the necessary capital to explore the creation of a flower business.

While Charles and Sarah were working, Faith was left with her maternal grandmother, Eliza Faith. Eliza Faith and her granddaughter had an unbreakable connection. They spent every moment together when Faith's parents were working. Eliza would frequently sing and tell bible stories to Faith. They would attend church together with Charles and Sarah. They would take frequent walks together in the rural setting where the family lived. Faith's best memory was the butterscotch cookies her grandmother loved to bake. It was as if Eliza had become a surrogate parent for Faith. This rearing continued until Faith got older and began junior high school. It was then that tragedy hit Faith again like a ton of cement.

After coming home from school, Faith wanted to tell her grandmother what had happened that day. She had won a spelling bee and received a small trophy and a blue ribbon. Nothing had ever happened to her like that before. She was so excited at the prospect of letting Eliza Faith know. Her grandmother would be so proud of her.

Entering the front door, her grandmother did not greet her like she usually did. Faith sensed something was terribly wrong. She searched all over the house. She could not find her grandmother anywhere.

Finally, she arrived at her grandmother's bedroom. The door was slightly ajar. Upon pushing open the door and passing into this room, she saw her grandmother sitting in her rocker. Her head was tilted back, and her eyes were closed. She asked her grandmother if she was ok.

There was no answer. As she approached, she felt her grandmother's forehead. It felt cold and clammy. For a child of such tender years, she was startled. Something was dreadfully wrong.

Even at such a young age, she was taught how to respond in this type of circumstance. After calling 911, she called her parents. Charles responded after a brief delay to take him off the line he had been working with. Sarah answered immediately. Both parents told Faith to stay calm and they would be home quickly.

Upon arrival, there was nothing the paramedics could do. Eliza Faith had died of old age. While Charles and Sarah were heartbroken, the trauma affected Faith the worst. She was devastated. Her life would never be the same. This trauma sank Faith into a very severe depression that would haunt her to this day.

Faith received intensive counseling after this ordeal. Sarah made plans to spend more time with Faith until her emotions settled. It was when she was

close to graduation from high school that she seemed to snap out of her sadness and return to her good-natured self. That was when she first met Gabe. When she first saw Gabe, Faith's interest was almost non-existent. Faith and Gabe were in the same class and received average grades. However, Faith's attitude toward Gabe changed when she was made fun of one day at school. Some of the more affluent girls began to poke fun at the simple attire Faith was wearing. Gabe intervened. He tried to defend Faith by merely saying that faith will provide what a person needs. He added that sometimes simple things in life are the very best. At that moment, Faith's heart was captured by this intervening monologue.

Shortly thereafter, Faith and Gabe started to date. Their relationship had become very romantic. Gabe would consistently buy her little things to show his affection. These items included trinkets and flowers.

Faith would often return the favor. She had learned how to cook her grandmother's butterscotch cookies. She would bring a batch to school that they would eat during their lunch recess. The severe depression that had affected Faith slowly started to dissipate.

While she was not completely over the death of her twin sister and her beloved grandmother, Faith's emotions moderated significantly with her relationship with Gabe. They became inseparable. Before graduation, Gabe would pick Faith up daily to take her to school. After doing their homework, they would venture out and have a burger or a Coke. On rare occasions, they would go to the restaurant where Sarah worked. Sarah would treat them to the daily special then resume her shift. All seemed to be well for Faith and Gabe.

Faith was like her mother. She never really had any long-range plans. Her only thought was to fill a void in her life resulting from her grandmother's death. She wanted so badly to get married and have children. She was content with waitressing after graduation. However, her fleeting thought was to help her mother at her flower shop when it would eventually open. Simple things were the only important things for Faith. By her grandmother's instruction, God and faith would provide all the comfort and answers that she needed.

A few years after their graduation, Faith and Gabe announced their engagement. Gabe was an auto mechanic. At that time, he was an assistant at his Uncle Stu's garage. With their work ethic, their financial struggles would gradually fade. They planned to build a modest nest egg, then start raising a family. Although they opted for a simple life, this type of life was suited to Faith and Gabe. They had so much love for each other.

Faith and Gabe got married five years ago. It was a simple ceremony with each immediate family member and a few friends in attendance.

Faith had begun helping her mother at her flower shop. Gabe continued working for his uncle. They had purchased a very small house on the outskirts of Nashville. Months later, all seemed nearly perfect when Faith had an announcement. She was a few months pregnant with her first baby.

Faith and Gabe were very excited at the prospect of having a child. They spent many hours after work contemplating baby names and creating a room for this blessing. Charles and Sarah also shared in the prospective joy of becoming grandparents. Charles said at this moment he had never seen Faith as happy as she was.

However, this emotion would not last. Like the formation of a rapid devastating storm, events occurred to shatter Faith's almost perfect life. These events happened a year to the day after Faith's marriage. On this day, she experienced sharp pains in her abdomen. These pains became more pronounced as the day progressed. Eventually, she noticed that she had been bleeding. With this alarming development, she called Gabe to take her to a local hospital emergency room.

All efforts were in vain. While Faith was fine, the efforts to save the baby went awry. Faith suffered an unexpected miscarriage. Doctors said it was created by a medical anomaly. In some way, a minor infection had worked its way to her cervix, inhibiting the growth of the fetus. The technical jargon the doctors used in explaining this rare phenomenon did little to quell the emotional anguish Faith and the family experienced with this news.

Faith was an emotional wreck upon learning of the miscarriage. Gabe tried to offer encouragement to her that life would get better. There was a reason why this happened. They could try again, follow doctors more carefully, and maintain their prayers. This was little consolation for Faith. Tragedies had now consumed her life on three occasions: the deaths of her twin, her grandmother, and now her very own baby. She had to return to counseling as a result of this upheaval in her life.

Charles told me that time has a way of trying to mend old wounds. After lengthy counseling sessions, a favorable attitude slowly started to permeate Faith's life again. She and Gabe continued their ideal relationship. She helped her mother at the flower shop. Her counseling helped provide distractions from the woes that had befallen her. As a result, Faith eventually got pregnant again.

While Faith remained anxious about her baby's health, she maintained vigils to pray daily. Her faith had become resounding. She would speak to her grandmother frequently. Likewise, she made frequent trips to her grave. Finally, she followed every specific instruction of her doctors. Gabe and her parents continued to nurture unrelenting love and support for her. The thought was that their bold willpower would make the result of her pregnancy different.

Almost nine months later, Faith gave birth to a very healthy baby boy. Faith and Gabe decided to name this child after the father and partly his maternal grandfather. His name was Gabriel Charles, Jr. This blessing did wonders to change Faith's emotion. She resumed the journey down the path for a contented and loving life with Gabe and Baby Gabe.

For three years, Faith was as content and happy as she had ever been. Her life was complete. Her little son made all the difference. The simple life of this simple family continued. The baby grew. Along with Gabe Jr., life within this family reached a pinnacle of fulfillment and serenity. However, a black cloud with the formation of a monstrous storm would again materialize over the horizon.

Baby Gabe had begun to experience health problems around the age of three. Faith first noticed he had been lethargic and unresponsive on occasion. As time progressed, this lethargy became more prevalent. He cried a lot as if he were experiencing pain. He seemed to run frequent fevers, failed to eat what Faith prepared, lost some weight, and had a paleness to his skin. After documenting these symptoms, Gabe suggested that they take Baby Gabe to the hospital.

The sadness that would then result almost took the life from Faith. After hearing the symptoms and running tests, the examining doctor conveyed the extremely bad news. Baby Gabe had developed an acute form of leukemia.

While the doctor tried to be optimistic, the nature of this illness, based on the tests provided little reason. The result of this illness was often fatal. After hearing this news, Faith and Gabe embraced and cried for the longest time. Charles stated that he almost lost his breath when he heard that dire news.

Approximately one month later, Baby Gabe succumbed to this illness. The family was heartbroken once again. Gabe initially began to develop a little distance from Faith. He felt as if he were the perpetrator bringing bad fortune to the marriage. Upon hearing this, Faith fought through her depression to tell him he was not to blame. He was as loving a husband and father as a wife and mother could ever dream of. She said if they fought together, they would be able to overcome these hardships and receive the blessings she thought they deserved.

When it rains, it pours. While trying to rebound from Baby Gabe's passing, Gabe started to have dizzy spells at work. His vision became blurry. His vision deteriorated to the point where he was no longer able to work. He had frequent headaches that medicines like aspirin were very slow or ineffective in alleviating. Sometimes, Gabe even had problems walking. At that moment, Faith asked God in prayer what was happening to her and her family. While Charles and Sarah provided financial support during this trying period, Faith was lost without the love of her life. The void of the loss of her grandmother, Eliza Faith, came back with a viciousness that threatened to cut Faith's very soul.

Charles and Sarah helped Faith take Gabe to the doctor. Tragedy sometimes has a way of striking twice. Based on the symptoms with a follow-up MRI, it was diagnosed that Gabe had a brain tumor. Faith's jaw just dropped. All she could do at that moment was cry. The doctors tried to reassure her that through treatments, some patients were able to overcome this type and location of tumor growth.

Initial treatments helped a little early on. Through time, the growth in Gabe's brain had little reaction to typical treatments. The doctors started to lose their bearings as to what to try next. At that time, Faith had read of an experimental treatment being worked on at the University of Phoenix. While this treatment showed some degree of effectiveness in sample patients, it had not undergone necessary trial studies in a large representative group of patients. As this treatment remained the family's only option, Charles and Sarah made plans to venture west the following morning. Gabe, however, would be flown there immediately.

I had a surprising encounter with this mysterious couple a few days later. My heart filled with sadness at all the facts of this story. Tears developed in my eyes thinking about all the pain and depression that must be clouding Faith's spirit. I tried to hold back the tears. The story had come full circle. At that moment, I drove over the last hill on the freeway, seeing the skyline of Nashville below me.

CHAPTER 9

The Apex of Faith's Misery

Clouds of depression formed in my mind, driving the distance from Memphis to Nashville. Faith's story had a profound impact on my heart. My only thought and prayer was to eventually meet with her. I wanted to convey to her that everything would work out. God has a way of turning positives out of what appeared to be hopeless negatives. However, arriving in Nashville slowly made the clouds dissipate. There was a renewed sense of excitement at the tasks I had to complete. Not only would I continue the journey to Knoxville, but I also had to focus on a visit to my grandparents' graves. I continued to need supplies. Finally, I was starting to feel my hunger subsume me because of a more consistent rumble in my stomach. I would have to temporarily push all other thoughts and emotions to the far recesses of my mind.

My first responsibility was to exit at a truck stop and top off my fuel. Upon arriving at this truck stop, I looked around at where my was. Several miles down the freeway was the locale of the Grand Ole Opry. Seeing a billboard for this historic venue brought back many memories of my youth. My grandparents took me to hear the remarkable country music showcased at this venue a few times when I was young. I remembered them saying prayers before and after our few journeys there. The music, the artists, and the acoustics left an indelible impression on me.

While seemingly simple, these trips provided incredible memories of how blessed I was as a child.

After fueling my rig, I decided to freshen up a bit to continue my trek. I purchased a coffee and a small doughnut to quell my growing appetite. I realized I needed to find a flower shop for the visit to my grandparents' cemetery. I knew a lot about Nashville.

However, I had no idea where the nearest flower shop was. As I was taking my phone from my pocket to attempt an internet search, I was distracted by the sound of a bird. I looked up and there I saw it.

Ahead of me on the street was a sign for S.J. Flowers, Bouquets and Gifts. This shop was only a few miles down the highway. I had the sense that God was directing me to this shop for some reason. The billboard had an attractive design. There was a woman holding an assorted bouquet of flowers with two similar-looking younger girls holding smaller bouquets. The girls almost appeared to be twins.

Because of the appeal of this ad, I felt that was where I needed to go. Upon arriving at this shop, I was fortunate to find a place to park my rig. As I exited the cab, I noticed a white Chevy Cavalier parked toward the rear of the parking area next to the building. While there were a few other vehicles, this is the car that seemed to stand out to me. After glancing there, I walked into the shop.

Inside the shop, there were a few customers quietly milling about. At that moment, I was approached by an older woman who appeared to be a manager. She introduced herself as Sarabeth. She had a gleaming personality and a sparkling smile. She also had glowing hazel eyes with short blonde hair. She had a striking resemblance to Sarah.

She inquired if I needed assistance. As I was about to tell her my desire, the phone on a nearby counter rang. She respectfully excused herself. Before answering the phone, she sent another associate to assist me.

This associate greeted me. As we made eye contact, I felt some extraordinary connection with this woman. However, since her name tag was turned around, I was unable to see what it said. She had her hair up, and her eyes seemed weary and tired as if she had been under much stress. However, her hair was remarkably like the hair that I saw when I briefly observed Miri in my encounters with her. Further, she also possessed radiant and sensitive blue eyes. I was in awe of her beauty and was left speechless.

I managed to tell this assistant what I desired. I was looking for a particular arrangement to place on my grandparents' graves. She expressed her sympathy. Then she managed to take me to a memorial display where I was able to choose the right arrangement. My grandparents undoubtedly would be proud of this arrangement and the attempt I was making to remember them. I almost asked for her name, but I was in a hurry. I simply thanked this assistant. Before I left, I heard Sarabeth tell her assistant that she could go after that transaction followed by a little cleaning. I was moved and felt something strange about this meeting. Did this meeting have some connection to all the other events I had been experiencing? What about her resemblance to Miri?

I returned to my truck and began driving in the direction of the truck stop. Across from the truck stop, I had noticed a large retail outlet at that intersection. This place would be the ideal stop to get much needed personal supplies along with important supplies for my rig. Once I purchased these items, I had a little time to relax and eat.

I was not in the retail store exceptionally long. I immediately organized the purchased items in the rear of the cab. After I got out and closed the door, I finished the lukewarm coffee I had purchased when I first arrived. At that moment, I would experience an incident that would forever change my life. I believe that somehow God had orchestrated this event with divine motivation.

As I was sipping my coffee, I glanced at the intersection and observed an enormous crash. A black van had passed quickly in front of me and sped through the red light. This van immediately struck the passenger door of a white Chevy Cavalier. The Chevy Cavalier spun around several times ejecting a female driver from the vehicle. She landed several feet from where I was standing at my rig. At first glance she did not appear to be moving or even conscious. My first thought was to question how anyone could have ever survived such a vicious wreck.

My adrenaline began pumping in earnest at this calamity. My first instinct was to approach this woman. I needed to make sure she was alive and breathing until help arrived. I would have to draw on all my experiences to render the aid she urgently required. I knew that God would provide the strength to deal with this adversity.

When I approached this woman, I realized that I had seen her before. She was the assistant at the flower shop. I could tell by her tattered clothing. Her name tag had been torn from her shirt and was laying several feet from her demolished car in the street. I also noticed a couple of bloodied necklaces stretched tightly around her neck: one was a cross, the other a small locket. She had cuts and abrasions to her forehead. I detected a more serious wound at her left side. I immediately checked for a pulse.

She was not breathing, and her heart stopped. After rapidly wrapping the wound at her side, I immediately began CPR. I had little time to analyze this situation. I had to rely on faith and my internal instincts.

My only focus was to get this woman to breathe and her heart beating again. When I first saw her, I felt an indescribable allure toward this woman. It was essential that I keep her alive until health professionals arrived to take over.

Before opening my law office, I worked very briefly for a kitchen at a correctional facility in northern Arkansas. This position would provide the finances to establish my law office. During my training, I learned the essentials of self-defense. This training was imperative in the event of an altercation with a prisoner. Most importantly, I received valuable instruction in life-saving techniques. I was certified to render CPR in life threatening situations.

In my attempt to save this unfortunate woman, I started with chest compressions. These compressions were followed by a couple of short breaths. I then checked her pulse again. No pulse. I continued this technique. More compressions. Short breaths. No pulse. More compressions. Even more short breaths. I checked again. Still no response. After what seemed to be an eternity, I continued my efforts. I thought my efforts were too late.

After a few minutes of CPR, I said a prayer. At that moment, I believe I was a witness to a miracle. Reaching for her wrist, I detected a small pulse. Her heartbeat was soft, but there was one. I also saw her eyes twitch as if she were trying to open them. My eyes started to develop tears. Faith had indeed answered my prayers.

At that moment, the paramedics arrived. They asked me the current status of this victim. I told them after a few minutes of CPR, I had managed to get a pulse. An older gentleman with a soothing voice said that he and his female partner would take over. The last thing he said to me was that I most likely had saved this woman's life.

I was in shock as I returned to my truck. I obviously was trying to digest what had just happened. So many things had been happening in my life lately that were difficult to explain. I longed to talk to Miri again. She may have the answers that I desired. Unfortunately, I needed to refocus on my trip to the cemetery as well as the completion of my haul.

I resumed driving toward Knoxville. Yet I was subsumed by thoughts of this woman. What was her name? Where was she going? In the flower shop, why did she look so sad and stressed? I would ponder these questions all the way to the cemetery. Since the accident affected my schedule, I no longer had the time to eat a big home-cooked meal. I had a load to pick up the next morning.

My plan was to exit at Cookeville, Tennessee after I drove over an hour. At that time, I wanted to stretch my legs, grab a fast meal, then continue toward Jamestown, Tennessee. Outside of Jamestown was the location of the cemetery I desperately wanted to visit. I also planned to call Charles and Sarah to inform them of the progress of my excursion.

Traffic became heavy as I reached the outskirts of Nashville. My head flooded with flashbacks to the accident victim. It was unfortunate I did not know her name. Moreover, I returned to thinking about Faith.

In the solitude of truck driving, I had many opportunities to think about various topics. I would be plagued by these thoughts all the way to Cookeville and eventually Jamestown.

Thoughts of Faith started to encompass my mind. She had endured so many hardships in her life. Her relationship with Gabe seemed to be crucial and uplifting. I wondered how she would manage to deal with the additional stress of his death. I felt this depression may lead to unnecessary tragedy.

I had experienced depression when I was employed at the prison. The feeling took a massive bite out of a mentor who had been training me. The trainer was a short Filipina woman in her mid-30s referred to as Ms. Santos. She seemed to always possess a smile and a positive demeanor. She openly answered any of my questions. She would always provide assistance whenever it was needed. I would have never guessed that a dark cloud was circulating around her like the mist encircling me in my dreams with Miri.

One day, I was summoned into the duty office for an information meeting. Something intense had to have happened for such protocol. It was then that I learned some tragic news. It would have a detrimental effect on me continuing to work at the prison. Soon thereafter, I left the prison. Additionally, it would be my first exposure to dealing with serious mental issues.

A few days before this meeting, Ms. Santos had been escorted out of the facility. She had been under investigation for intimate personal contact with an inmate. This alleged contact was a violation of prison personnel policy as well as a violation of the law. She would not be allowed to return until after the completed investigation. Afterwards, a decision would be made concerning her employment along with the inevitability of her being subject to criminal charges.

Ms. Santos appeared to be under a great deal of stress. The magnitude of this stress was not apparent to those surrounding her. I had no forewarning of what was transpiring. Not only did she have problems at the prison, but she also had financial problems and boyfriend woes at home. With the nature of these issues, she was on a collision course with catastrophe.

The prison warden informed us that this stress was insurmountable for Ms. Santos. The prior afternoon she had access to a firearm.

Thinking that death was her only answer, she put the gun to her head and pulled the trigger. It was the only time in my life that I had been exposed to a suicide. In the back of my mind, I always questioned whether I could have said or done anything to have induced a different outcome. Only God would have that answer. I know I was determined to prevent such a tragedy from occurring again.

With the depression Faith had clearly experienced, I questioned whether this avenue would be a possibility with her. Based on what Charles told me, she appeared to have the strength to overcome her heartache. However, I would have emerging doubts with the quality of tragedies in her life. She would be all alone now. I was determined not to let these tragedies disintegrate her being like those in the life of Ms. Santos.

Once I resolved these thoughts, I had arrived in Cookeville. I pulled over in a supermarket parking lot. I needed to relax and focus again. Soon I would be in Jamestown visiting the cemetery. I was sure I would get emotional as a flood of memories of my youth would catapult to the fore. My grandparents and I had a special bond.

During this break, I retrieved my phone. I tried calling Charles and Sarah. The first time the phone just rang. I tried again. The second time I was able to get through to their voicemail. I left a message for them. My initial thought was that they were planning for Gabe's funeral. At that moment, I renewed my focus on the trip to my grandparents' graves.

An hour later, I arrived in Jamestown. My thoughts refocused solely on the lives of my grandparents. Tears started to fall on my cheek as I pulled into the cemetery. I was choked up and at a loss as to what to say. In my heart, I truly missed the comfort and companionship of my grandparents. They did a great deal to instill my sound faith in God.

I stopped the truck, exited, retrieved the flowers, and began walking toward their graves. It had been years since I had visited this little cemetery. It was not very big. The grounds had been well kept. It was a serene locale as I could hear the wind blowing through my hair. Soon I arrived at their resting place.

I said a few words and prayed over their graves. After the prayer, I placed the arrangement near their headstones. I closed my eyes and meditated for a moment. Just when I thought my life was calm, I had another vision as I looked up.

I saw a figure on a little hill by a fence overlooking the cemetery. This figure looked familiar. I rubbed my eyes as I walked slowly in that direction. As I proceeded closer, I began to make out the figure. It was the same older woman I had seen at the cross. Again, I thought the stress may have been inducing a hallucination.

Moving closer, she appeared to mouth a couple of words to me. At the same moment, she reached out her arms like she wanted to hug me. Like my second visit to the cross, I was startled at this event. The words she appeared to mutter without sound were to thank me. I did not have a clue why she would be behaving this way.

Trying to restore my faculties, I was interrupted by the ringing of my phone. At that moment, the vision disappeared. On the phone was Charles. I did not have an opportunity to really speak. He stated he did not have much time. Yet he needed to tell me something important.

With a crackle to his voice, he stated that Faith was in the hospital. He was only able to say that she was in a serious accident earlier in the day. He concluded by saying he would keep me informed when he knew something and was able. At that moment, the call dropped.

I could not believe the contents of that call. The news was devastating. Tears developed and rolled down my cheeks. The apex of Faith's misery continued. It started with the death of her grandmother. Thereafter, her depression amplified with her miscarriage followed with the deaths of her Baby Gabe then her husband Gabe. I asked God why this woman was having to endure so much pain and loss. Did she deserve all of this heartache?

Was she being punished for some unforeseen reason? I knew I had to eventually return to Nashville to see her. As I drove away from the cemetery, a distant thought entered the recesses of my mind: Could the accident victim have been Faith herself? Only time, God, and faith would provide the answer.

CHAPTER 10

A New Apparition in the Mist

The Journey to Knoxville

God frequently sends subtle yet obvious clues to the divine purpose He tries to convey. The observer merely needs to register the facts. Otherwise, the tendency is to overanalyze. God clearly was prodding me down a divine path. Maybe I was making events harder to understand than necessary. This understanding was apparent in my longing to meet Faith.

Leaving Jamestown en route to Knoxville, I began to reassess words and happenings since my initial contact with Miri. In our first meeting, she told me God would be providing significant changes in my life. I needed to trust my faith. She also mentioned that God would bring what I longed for and lacked during my life. I would need to pay attention to the signs that were placed in front of me. In the end, the reasons should be obvious to me.

I left the stability of my law practice to escape Jennifer's mental fragility. I began my career as a truck driver to help create distance between Jennifer and me. I had been plagued by the consistent anxieties she possessed which were detrimental to our lives. My encounter with Miri reinforced the thought that there was something better out there for me. I was hopeful that the void of companionship in my life would ultimately be filled with true love and respect.

The multiple visions I had experienced achieved a bright clarity at that moment. The old woman at the cross directed me to go east. In New Mexico, I encountered the Jennings couple. I thought about how this family lived in Nashville. I learned that they had a daughter whose many heartaches cast her into a bleak depression. Working through my loneliness, a female voice beckoned me. The billboard I perceived stated that faith would provide the answers I sought. I recalled Faith's recent tragedy with Gabe and how she must now be alone. When Charles informed me of her accident, my only assumption was that she had to be as depressed as ever. I had more desire to meet and talk to her than I ever did.

In our second meeting, Miri told me that the immediate future would answer my questions. Prior contacts would assist me in recognizing the solution. I remembered again what Charles said when we last spoke.

Upon the mention of the accident involving Faith, I instantly began to ponder whether Faith and the accident victim I had saved were, in reality, one and the same. I wish that I had just seen the name tag on the flower shop associate. That trivial observation would have provided answers to my inquiries. I needed to meet Faith to verify this emerging thought. I had to return to Nashville.

There would remain unanswered questions. Who exactly was Miri? Miri also intimated in the second dream that someone close to her was about to experience another tragedy. Who was this person, and how were they connected? Was it even conceivable that Miri and Faith were connected in some way? Who was the old woman at the cross I encountered on two occasions? Was she the same old woman I saw when I visited my grandparents' graves? Who was the younger woman I saw when I was in Ontario, talking to Crystal? I tried to be patient, but the anxiety of not knowing began to overcome me. In the end, I said a prayer that God would place the pieces of this puzzle together in an overwhelming portrait of understanding.

At that moment, I had arrived in Knoxville. Following my GPS, I arrived at the gate through which to enter to pick up my load. This building had several open loading docks. I received the dock number for my load assignment. Immediately thereafter, I backed my trailer into this open dock for the loading of the retail art supplies. It did not take long for a couple of forklift drivers to safely load the pallets into my trailer. I pulled out my rig and headed to a nearby truck stop to rest for the evening.

Another eventful day had passed. I had not heard anything else from Charles and Sarah. As I was setting my alarm to rise early the next morning, I was worried about Faith's health. Was she still alive? Was she improving? What was the state of her mental health? What about the victim I saved? What was her status? I continued having flashbacks to the accident. I was reliving every moment of the day. Fortunately, with the soft Christian music in the background, I eventually fell into a deep sleep.

Faith Appears in the Mist?

I was limp as I felt a coolness around my body. I got up and started walking again. Gradually, my eyes opened wide. I began to outline what I was seeing around me. I once again found myself walking in the mist. I felt a sense of relief as I tried to get Miri to answer the questions that had grown to torment my spirit.

I first noticed the path. It was becoming all too familiar with my experience in the mist. Yet I sensed something different about this journey. Initially, I was unable to pinpoint exactly what was amiss.

I observed my familiar surroundings. I heard the bubbling brook and the birds in the distance. However, I also heard what sounded like a low hum coming from my left. I had not heard this hum before. This sound was some distance away from the brook and the path I was navigating. I could only form assumptions as I had little time or patience to investigate. I had to locate Miri.

I did think the hum was coming from some type of building. I could faintly make out lights coming from a small hill in the distance. I remembered that I had heard a similar sound recently. With my journey and my consistent stress, I could not remember where I had heard it.

The noise reminded me of a sound one would hear walking outside a commercial building in and around a city. I would dwell on this sound as I continued walking.

Eventually, I arrived at the gazebo. I was startled when I saw it was encompassed by darkness. The only light emanating from the vicinity was from the full moon hovering overhead. I looked around, but I did not see Miri. The gazebo was empty. Miri was not there. I tried yelling for her. There was no response. Where was Miri?

I continued walking down the path. The mist had subsided when I reached the gazebo. The mist continued to fade as I passed the bench Miri and I occupied during my trips there. However, the farther I walked, the more the mist began to materialize again. I was full of anxiety now as to what to expect. There appeared to be no one around.

Just when I thought my attempts to find Miri were in vain, I began to observe another figure in the mist. At first sight, it was difficult to make out specific characteristics of this apparition. Only as I got closer was I able to discern that it was a person. Advancing even closer, the image of a female was walking toward me.

Initially, I thought this female stranger was not a stranger at all. Outlining her face, she had a similar face and hairstyle to Miri. However, she voiced some words to me. These words were in a southern drawl that I had not heard before. Miri's voice never sounded that way. Miri's dialect sounded very different.

As we arrived several feet from each other, I noticed cuts and abrasions on her face. I also noticed she was wincing in apparent pain when she walked. I realized that she was wearing a shirt that appeared to have been torn. A place in her pocket was ripped. This appeared to be a location where a person would pin a name badge. Immediately, my thought was to identify this person as the one I rescued from the violent accident. I had to ask her for her name.

I realized my time here with her was running short when lightning appeared close to where we were standing. The sound of thunder was familiar. It was also within a short distance from both of us. The female stranger seemed startled and scared at the sound. Only then did she ask me to help her. Her face seemed to be worn and stressed. However, I sensed a genuine relief in her eyes when I grabbed her hands and asked her to sit on the nearest bench. I told her my name was Frank.

She said she had many questions. Where was she? What happened? She only remembered that she had been driving when her mind faded to darkness. She asked if I knew what happened. Before I had a chance to respond, she continued with a series of more questions followed by an enlightening statement.

She remembered being very depressed at events in her life. Within a short period, her heart had been beset with some tragedies. These events had taken their toll. However, she was unable to elucidate these events. Unquestionably, she was likely experiencing some form of amnesia.

She added that this depression had consumed her spirit. She was questioning why she was the only one alive while others she loved had died. Even as life was improving, another tragedy would intervene with a tightening grip. She wondered why she should even go on living.

I was taken aback by these comments. However, I reached deep into the faith and inspiration that helped soothe my heart in times like these. I explained that she had every reason to live. I asked her to look around. Did she not hear the sound of the serene bubbling brook? Did she not perceive the sound of the birds chirping in the distance? She took an interest in my comments and stared directly into my eyes.

I told her that her life would only improve as long as she had faith. She smiled widely when I said that. I added an inspirational verse from the bible. This verse came from Isaiah:

Fear you not; for I am with you: be not dismayed; for I am your God:
I will strengthen you; yes, I will help you; yes, I will uphold you with the
right hand of my righteousness.
Isaiah 41:10.

This stranger gripped my hands tightly. I could sense that some of the stress was leaving her body as tears began forming in our eyes.

I continued by explaining some of my background. I had also experienced upheaval and tragedy. I described how I came from a loving family, and my parents had died unexpectedly. I also spent time with my grandparents. They, too, had died abruptly. I described how they told me bible verses and spent a great deal of time teaching inspiration and faith. I briefly mentioned the trips taken to Nashville's Grand Ole Opry. At that moment, she gripped my hands tightly.

Despite the tragedies, this inspiration fueled my mental well-being and the health of my body and spirit.

As the thunder and lightning were so close now, I was about to conclude with words concerning my turbulent marriage to Jennifer. I was going to mention how I struggled with her anxiety and mental health. I did not get an opportunity. The thunder sounded like a bomb detonating next to us. I released her hands and told her we had to leave. Reluctantly, she understood. I departed in the direction from which I came. She began to walk toward the mist. I yelled for her not to worry. We would meet again.

She would be fine. I would help see her through her misfortunes. Her life would improve if she just allowed faith to lend a hand. As she was about to disappear into the mist, she took one final look at me. She smiled. She had a few last words. She said her name was Faith. At that moment, everything turned to darkness again.

CHAPTER 11

The Search for Faith

My Return to Nashville

I awoke early the next morning to the sound of my phone. However, this time the noise was not my alarm. I had been sent a text message. Wiping the sleep from my eyes, I squinted to read this note.

The text had been sent by Charles. He indicated that he was apprehensive about having time to meet with me. He was very concerned about Faith's life. Overnight, he and Sarah almost witnessed another significant tragedy.

After Faith arrived at the hospital, she occupied a room in the intensive care unit. She had undergone several hours of surgery to stop some internal bleeding. Her condition was very serious and life-threatening. Charles added that a few hours ago, Faith's vital signs had disappeared completely on two occasions. On both occasions, her doctors administered CPR with a mild shock. With these efforts, these doctors recovered her vital signs. While she appeared to be stabilizing, her attending physician remained pessimistic. Her weakness from stress was the indeterminate factor in predicting her survival. Charles concluded by typing that he and Sarah would be at the hospital all day. Charles must have been heartbroken with this information.

On my way to Oklahoma City, I needed to stop in Nashville. I needed to find Faith. She appeared so discouraged when I observed her in the mist. I wanted to tell her that old memories could be replaced by new and even better memories. I felt I had deserted Jennifer in her battles to overcome anxiety. The potential consequences of deserting Faith were far more serious. I was determined to see Faith through this chaotic time.

However, my life became easier knowing Faith and the woman in the accident were the same person.

I commenced my routine to undertake another day of driving. I quickly went into the truck stop to take a shower and get dressed. I stared into the mirror. At that time, a pertinent question popped into my mind. Because of their facial similarities, could Miri and Faith be related in some way? The more absurd thought was whether the two could be the same person. I dismissed this thought as their dialects were different. As these thoughts were fleeting, they exited my mind just as promptly as they entered.

With a doughnut and coffee at my side, I started driving to Nashville. This drive would take approximately three hours. I thought it would take even longer since there was a cool, dense fog permeating the area. I would have plenty of time to formulate my agenda. I would have many questions when I found Faith. Yet I would not be able to spend much time with her. I had to deliver my load to the Oklahoma City facility the next day.

I also needed to tell Faith additional facts about my past. I was going to mention Jennifer when the thunder and lightning overwhelmed us. I wanted to reassure her that everything would work out. She would be happy and healthy again. We both had so much to live for. I wanted to be her anchor in her volatile ship of life.

As I drove, the hills of Tennessee overtook my heart. Traversing the countryside, a jumble of thoughts flooded my head. I turned on my Christian music to soothe my spirit. Yet the thoughts continued to come.

I thought about Charles and Sarah. They, too, had experienced great heartache over the years. First, Sarah's mother died unexpectedly. Faith was there to witness this devastating adversity. The stress of handling Faith's depression must have been enormous. Dealing with Gabe's tragic passing following the miscarriage and the death of Baby Gabe was a great test of their faith. Now, with the accident, Faith's life was thrown into the mix. I had to make the effort to empathize more to soothe their spirit. Because of their temperament, they did not deserve this misfortune. I was confident their lives would improve with time.

Finally, I thought about Jennifer. I was filled with sadness concerning my inability to help her. Her anxiety had overwhelmed me. Maybe the severity of her condition amplified itself because I had never experienced anything like it. I had to be more sensitive to mental illness and its causes and treatments.

Since I would be passing through Little Rock, I needed to contact Jennifer. With the divorce pending, I needed to check the status. I wanted to convey the location where she could send any future correspondence. Most importantly, I needed to check to see if life was better for her and her new boyfriend. I owed it to her as well as myself to maintain cordial relations with a person I continued to think highly of. I also did not forget her two darling children. I am sure they felt confused by the turmoil surrounding my split with Jennifer.

Traffic started to get heavier as I approached Nashville. For a brief time, I was caught in a serious traffic jam. Traffic on both sides of the freeway was slowed or stopped for several miles. There was a truck accident in front of me that had snarled all lanes of the freeway. At that moment, I recalled my effort to save Faith. As frustration set in, I knew this would subtract time from my ability to see Faith and her family. However, with the Christian music playing, I started singing.

This impromptu karaoke-like behavior served to alleviate my anxiety and impatience. A calmness overtook my heart.

After a prayer, the freeway was once again moving smoothly. I would be in Nashville shortly. I was looking forward to a rest break. Although I was not very hungry, I needed to eat a little. Afterwards, I had much to do in a short time while I visited the city.

As the skyline of the city approached, I mentally outlined my itinerary once I stopped. First and foremost, I had to find Faith. I had no idea where to start. I had to call Charles. He would provide the answers I was desperate for. He could simply provide the name of the hospital. After resolving the main issue, I pulled into the first truck stop I found after exiting in Nashville. I would have less than an hour to accomplish my objectives.

Efforts to Find Faith

Once at the truck stop, I quickly entered and purchased a small sub and a soft drink. As I sat in my truck, I tried to call Charles. The phone merely rang on my first effort. Trying again, I was able to access his voicemail. I informed him that I was in town. I needed to find Faith. I needed to know the name of her hospital. I could only eat, drink, and wait for a response.

After ten minutes without a response, I sent him a text message. To visit with Charles, Sarah, and Faith, I needed to know where to find them. I told him it was urgent. I had little time before I would have to continue my journey to Oklahoma City. I would be heartbroken if I could not see all of them. At a minimum, I needed to check into Faith's condition directly. I concluded by texting that I was saying continuous prayers for the health and safety of Faith and her family.

I waited. I finished my meal. I received no response. I waited a little longer. My phone remained quiet. My anxiety was reaching a serious level. I was running out of time to try to find Faith. I resorted to the one behavior that had comforted me during such moments. I said a simple and succinct prayer. If I were meant to find Faith, then God would reach His mighty hand and carry me to her.

Observing my phone, I thought I would search for hospitals around the area. Maybe this search would provide a clue as to how I could find Faith. Sadly, the search revealed approximately seven area hospitals. I could eliminate some of these facilities. One was a children's hospital. Another was specifically a burn trauma center. However, at least five hospitals remained on my list. I did not have the time or patience to call each hospital individually. Additionally, since I was not family, I really had doubts as to what information the hospitals would provide for me. They may only be able to indicate whether Faith was an admitted patient.

I had to do something else. I no longer had any time to spare. Only a few minutes would remain for me to try to see Faith. I said a very short prayer for an immediate answer and comfort. Tears started to form in my eyes. A couple managed to stream down my cheeks. Almost instantaneously, I looked in front of me and I noticed a billboard. It was an ad for the same flower shop: S.J. Flowers, Bouquets and Gifts.

Hastily, I thought that someone there might have the answer to where Faith was. After all, she was apparently an associate there.

I quickly started my rig and proceeded in the direction of that flower shop. It would not take very long. The billboard provided directions. It was only four exits ahead of me on the freeway toward west Nashville. My excitement started to build. I perceived that by noticing the billboard, God was providing the answer I needed.

Soon, I arrived at the flower shop. I was shocked at what I found. There were no vehicles in the parking area. For that time of day and season, I thought that the lot would be modestly full of patrons.

Although some holidays like Easter had passed, Memorial Day was approaching. Yet I parked my rig and noticed no one entered or left this shop.

Moments later, I would see the reason. Arriving at the door, I saw a notice taped to its window. The writing seemed to be rushed as if someone was in a hurry. This note merely stated that the shop would be closed until further notice. There had been a family emergency requiring the utmost attention. The note concluded by expressing apologies for having to close. At the end were the following handwritten initials: S.J.

My sadness hit me like a brisk Arctic wind blowing after a severe snowstorm. I did not realize that this young woman and her life had made such an impact on my heart. I was at a loss for what to do. Time had run out for me. I could not stay in Nashville. I had to begin my journey to deliver the load to Oklahoma City. My job was dependent on the timely delivery of the loads. There would be serious consequences for undue delay, including reduction of pay, disciplinary action, and termination. I would have to return to Nashville at a later time.

I started my truck and began the slow drive toward the freeway.

Soon, I entered the interstate on my way out of Nashville. It was impossible at that point to contain my emotions. I was almost bawling like a hungry baby. Slowly, I said a few more prayers. I started listening to my Christian songs again. An eerie calm possessed my spirit. At that moment, I understood that being patient meant surrendering everything to God. Leaving the outskirts of Nashville, I understood it may be a painful march. Yet ultimately, at the end of that march, God would provide the triumph that faith required.

CHAPTER 12

Never Doubt God's Direction

Leaving Faith

As I continued driving out of Nashville, I was hopeful that God would provide some direction concerning how to find Faith. After seeing her in the mist, I needed an update concerning her condition. I remained confident that God would furnish the answers. It was hard for me to understand that He would only respond in His time according to His own terms.

Something about that surreal moment in the mist seemed to bring me closer to Faith. She had begun to fulfill a need: to fill the void of companionship I desperately required with the loss of my parents and the impending divorce to Jennifer. My heart ached at the thought of losing Faith. Was this the blossoming seed of true love that I desperately sought? Only God and time would hold the truth.

Silence permeated my truck as another inexplicable event occurred.

As I was deep in my meditation, I saw a faint and hazy image of a young woman materialize in front of my windshield. It happened so quickly that I had difficulty realizing whether I even saw it. She resembled Miri. She quickly pointed to my right. She disappeared almost as soon as she appeared. Briefly looking away from the road, I noticed a billboard.

The ad vividly displayed a hospital with a cancer unit attached. I was startled at this sight.

Even though I concentrated on driving, I did have the opportunity to mentally digest the specific contents of this sign. The hospital had a fascinating architectural design. This image was a photo of the main building beside another building, which housed the cancer unit. A covered walkway connected the two buildings. Even more enlightening was a path that led past both buildings down a hill toward a more serene location. The path appeared next to a little stream. Along this path, I noted small benches spread intermittently along the way. I was shocked to discern a white gazebo midway along this route. I had the eerie sensation that I had been on this path. Was this the path in the mist where I met Miri and Faith?

Relying on the words Miri had provided about following God's direction, my heart told me this facility must be the place where Faith was. The name of the hospital was St. John's Memorial Hospital and Cancer Treatment Center. I remembered the address. The hospital was located on the east side of Nashville. Surprisingly, the location was only a few blocks from the Grand Ole Opry.

I knew then that I eventually had to return to Nashville. With this sign, I knew where Faith was. Every sign I had experienced led me to pursue this connection. I simply needed to know she was recovering. I wanted to have an impact on her life. At that moment, I felt comforted and started listening to another Christian music CD.

Feelings of anticipation replaced the sweeping presence of sadness. My only thought was to deliver my load and take some time off. A few days around Faith may just be what both of us would require. Immediately, I prayed that God would restore Faith's health. Since I had not heard from Charles about Faith's health, anxiety was slowly creeping into my heart.

Traffic increased significantly as I approached Memphis. The first leg of this excursion was nearly at its end. I planned a brief stop. I had a couple of tasks warranting my attention. I remained on a strict schedule to arrive in Oklahoma City.

I tried calling Charles the moment I pulled into an east Memphis truck stop. I became flustered when there was no answer. However, simultaneous events occurred. It could only be God dictating life's course. My phone rang as I set it on the passenger seat.

Charles was finally calling me. He apologized for his lack of response. He added that he regretted not meeting with me. I said I understood. He had more pressing thoughts on his mind.

Moreover, he had important news. Ever since the last resuscitation efforts, Faith's vital signs had consistently improved. Her attending physician was amazed. He anticipated that shortly, she would be awake again. Charles mentioned that an angel must have arrived in her slumber, compelling her to fight to regain her health. I conveyed my relief at this news.

However, Charles added some additional unexpected news that happened just after she had been resuscitated the second time. While in Faith's room, Charles had almost nodded off. It was then he heard a voice. He quickly opened his eyes. He glanced at Faith. While still nearly comatose, she appeared to be mumbling a name. Since he could not decipher Faith's words, Sarah interjected what she heard. She was calling for Frank.

Charles was astonished. He asked himself how Faith would even know that name. My name had yet to be discussed in a conversation with his daughter. With a puzzlement I easily detected, Charles kept asking how she would know me.

Finally, Charles quickly added that he was eternally grateful. When I asked why, I felt lightheaded. I could not believe what I was hearing.

He wanted to let a kind nameless gentleman know that he appreciated this man's life-saving aid. When Faith first got into the car wreck, an older paramedic had revealed a bystander hastily performed CPR. Without this initial assistance, Faith would have surely died. As I was about to interject what happened that day, the phone line went dead.

Needless to say, I felt real surprise with this latest comment. I finally absorbed the fact I had indeed saved Faith's life. However, I did lose the chance to tell Charles. I would have told him I did what faith and compassion demanded.

The Puzzle Slowly Comes Together

I started my engine to resume my journey. I realized the way the pieces of the puzzle were fitting together. However, the puzzle was only partially finished. During the drive to Little Rock, all my thoughts centered on my recent past. The way the masterpiece was developing would dictate the course of my future.

The signs I had experienced had a common theme. I needed to find faith. I needed to go east. The direction of my life would be the product of this instruction. God would reveal the answers for the remedy for my heartache and loneliness. I did indeed find Faith. However, I never imagined she was a person rather than a concept.

An unbreakable bond formed between Faith and me. I knew of her past and her struggles. Likewise, I was aware of my own. I rescued her from a certain death. I sincerely thought there must be a divine reason for this chosen path. Saving someone's life created an indelible and indescribable bond without comparison. I remained excited as to the additional answers God would convey.

I thought about why Faith was calling my name. In some way, she must have met me while she was unconscious and dying. She did lose her vital signs on two occasions. At the same time, we both appeared in the mist. I could not discern any other explanation.

Using this reasoning, Miri must have been an actual person. Yet Miri must have died. Did she exist from my past or Faith's past? I even had another questionable but fleeting assessment. Was it even possible Miri could be the twin sister Faith had lost shortly after her birth? I was inclined to deduce she was linked to Faith. The older woman I had seen must also be someone from Faith's past. But who were these women?

The drive to Little Rock was uneventful. My only observation was a couple of cars broken down by the freeway. Traffic was light. The weather was pleasant. Before I realized I was there, I was pulling into a rest area near Little Rock.

At this rest stop, I slapped some cold water on my face. I purchased some strong coffee from a vending machine. When I returned to my truck, I retrieved my phone. I sent a text to Jennifer. I wanted to check the status of our divorce. Finally, I concluded by indicating I would establish a temporary post office box in Little Rock. I would check this box for important correspondence. I then continued my trek.

A very short time later, I stopped at a truck stop after driving past a few more exits. Nearby, I noticed a small post office. Since it was open, I quickly entered. I was able to obtain the temporary post office box. I sent a last text to Jennifer to confirm this information. I had completed my last task. Oklahoma City was five hours away.

I quickly returned to the freeway. I was optimistic that I would arrive in Oklahoma City at a decent hour. I wanted to get sufficient rest to deliver my load. I had to request time off so I could return to Nashville. Meeting Faith in person was my ultimate priority. All my concentration was on this quest. The five-hour drive quickly became four. Then it turned into three.

All this time, I thought of the minute details of the experiences I encountered as a truck driver. However, there was one little detail that jumped into my consciousness. It concerned the flower shop.

During my legal career, I developed a rational and logical thought process. Every experience seemed to be interwoven with some kind of mental structure. The name of the flower shop entered my awareness. The flower shop where I encountered Faith was named S.J. Flowers, Bouquets and Gifts. I studied those initials. I then thought about the mysterious couple that quickly had turned into my good friends. Sarah Jennings had the same initials. I learned from Charles that she desired her own flower shop. It was there that I met Faith. This undoubtedly had to be her flower shop. Her only ambition was to open this type of business. Faith always wanted to help her mother. While I did not know the correlation of Sarabeth in the unresolved picture, I was able to deduce she must be related to the family because she had similar facial features and demeanor as I experienced with Sarah. Why could I not piece this together earlier?

I knew I was on the right path. God was directing me along this path with a divine objective. I would consistently have additional theories as I continued driving. God had overwhelmed my life with different events and occurrences for me to analyze and formulate reasons. However, continuing deep in thought, the three hours quickly turned into one.

With little traffic and perfect weather conditions, I arrived in Oklahoma City in record time. I was tired but elated that I had finally made it. I had finished my second run.

I turned into a truck stop near the location of the industrial facility housing the retail art supplies. The facility also stored paint for retail painting outlets. I was relieved to finally be able to relax. My day had been long. I was ready for a decent rest. I safely backed into a secluded area of the truck stop. As a creature of habit, I set my alarm. At that moment, I visualized the face and appearance of Faith. Despite her injuries, there was an allure that drew me even closer to her. After a brief moment with that thought, I fell into a much-needed sleep.

CHAPTER 13

The Call from Faith

Sunshine Provides a Short Leave

Faith has guided me along a remarkable path during my life. God has wanted me to live and learn. I was very blessed to be raised in a compassionate and caring environment. I had loving parents and grandparents. I was furnished with a good education with good morals.

Visions of Faith with her tragedies entered my mind. I longed to have her along on this exceptional journey. She needed someone stable and faithful like me to lift her through the chaotic events of her uncertain life. More importantly, I needed someone as sincere, faithful, and loving as she was.

Commencing my daily routine, I mentally planned my schedule for the day. First and foremost, I had to safely deliver my load. Following this delivery, I needed to contact Sunshine Logistics to request some time off. I was unsure of the nature and extent the company would honor this request. With the country's economic upheaval, drivers were essential in maintaining the continued functioning of pertinent market deliveries. The standards for Sunshine Logistics drivers were even higher.

Before long, I arrived at the appropriate dock at the paint facility. I backed in, opened the heavy rear doors, and allowed the workers to access the pallets. Like the regular beat of a drum, the pallets were removed and placed inside the plant. My trailer was emptied almost as soon as I opened the doors. Finally, I closed my doors, thanked the plant personnel, and returned to the nearby truck stop.

I developed genuine apprehension about my next task. Since it was my first request for time off, I did not know how management would handle this request. I waited. Shortly, I received another direct deposit into my bank account from Sunshine. Another text followed with a new load assignment: a load from Mobile, Alabama, to deliver to Atlanta, Georgia. Even though this request was for a short delivery, my thoughts centered on Faith and her condition.

Almost immediately, I called my driver manager, Thomas. He quickly answered the phone. After identifying myself, he expressed his sincere appreciation for the job I had been doing. I was punctual in both my pickups and deliveries. I was practicing safety as per the company's manual for drivers. No significant adverse comments existed in my file. However, once I mentioned I wanted time off, silence developed on the line.

After a few moments of this silence, Thomas inquired as to how long I would need. I told him some of the specifics about Faith and her injuries. While I desired at least a couple of weeks, I cut that period in half to approximately one week. I merely wanted to see her condition stabilize and her mental health improve. Thomas eventually answered that the company could only provide three days, excluding today and the following day, to head for my next load assignment. Although this was hard for him to agree to, he stated clearly that the company standards and continuity of my work were uppermost considerations.

I reluctantly agreed to the few days he would allow me. At least I would be able to travel to see Faith. I would be able to talk to Charles and Sarah. I would learn more about their family. Finally, I would understand what I would need to do to improve their lives after all they had undergone. Thomas typed this request on his computer. He finally added that I needed to check for a load assignment on the fourth day starting tomorrow. I told him I was grateful and that I would consistently check in with him.

Afterwards, apprehension was replaced by an intense excitement that I would be returning immediately to Nashville. I was just over nine hours from my destination. Circumstances would extend this period should I make any stops or experience any unforeseen delays. I was optimistic I would be able to visit Faith briefly before time slipped away from me this evening. I said a specific prayer for God to look after Faith and her family. My final thought was to pray that God would keep me sheltered and out of harm's way. It was then that I headed away from the truck stop.

Discovery of the Mysterious Hum

All during my travels, I was discovering the answers to questions put in front of me. I needed to go east. To venture east was to go to Nashville. To find answers to problems about me and life was to find Faith. Maybe to find the true love eluding me during my lifetime was to pursue this unexpected relationship.

I retraced my steps to get to this point. I relived the images, especially the times in the mist with Miri. These encounters were followed by saving Faith's life, meeting her in the mist, and her calling my name. Charles even conveyed his appreciation for the unknown man administering CPR. He had saved his precious little girl's life.

Knowing the impact of these events brought chills up and down my spine. Nothing was more valuable and breathtaking than knowing I had developed some bond or favor with God.

As I proceeded on the freeway toward Fort Smith, Arkansas, I resumed listening to my Christian music. This music had been very soothing during these driving adventures. I became even more relaxed when I started singing the songs. I was blessed to have that source of entertainment to keep me company.

During my musical interlude, I experienced road construction and slower traffic near Fort Smith. As a result, my mind started to wander to the meeting in the mist with Faith. Specifically, my heart returned to a sound I had heard before our encounter. What was causing the sound of the mysterious hum?

As I was trying to retrieve information from the files in my mind, I suddenly remembered. I had heard this sound when I dropped off Charles and Sarah.

The sound was emanating from the Phoenix hospital. I thought the sound was either from the heating/cooling unit or from the kitchen. The sound may have also had its origins from some kind of generator. Notwithstanding its source, it became obvious to me. The hospital was the location of this strange sound.

Armed with this information, I felt little doubt I was on the right track to find Faith. The hospital billboard I had seen vividly illustrated the connected buildings. Moreover, the path was a short distance from the hospital. I was on this path when I first heard the hum. Later, I would eventually encounter Faith. There was no doubt in my mind that St. John's was the hospital treating Faith.

My excitement increased astronomically with this understanding. At the same time, I drove beyond any traffic impediments. While I had to slow briefly through the Fort Smith vicinity, soon my speed once again became fast and steady. Any reduction in the time when I would arrive in Nashville would be minimal. My thoughts once again were aimed at Faith and the time we held hands on the bench in the mist. I carried this thought during the two-hour drive to Little Rock.

Jennifer's Last Endearing Letter

During my driving career, I had yet to experience any serious inclement weather. I drove mainly through pleasant and sunny conditions. I did encounter some brief intermittent downpours in Oklahoma and Texas on my way to Knoxville. That good fortune was about to change.

Strong showers and thunderstorms were prevalent as I was an hour from Little Rock. At times, the deluge was so heavy I thought I needed to pull over. However, my desire to visit Faith prodded me on. Traffic remained very slow as I entered Little Rock. These conditions made it certain that my estimated arrival time in Nashville would be later. I said a soft prayer that God would provide patience in understanding how to deal with the delay created by these storms.

I had a small task in Little Rock. I briefly stopped at the post office. My reason was merely to get out of the storms. My hope was that these storms would diminish when I was ready to depart. However, as I checked my box, I did not expect to find any mail. Toward the rear, I found a solitary letter.

I had no doubt who had sent this correspondence. Jennifer was the only person I notified about the post office box. I took the letter and returned to my truck. In the quiet confines of the cab, I slowly read what she had written. Surprisingly, the contents brought both an unexpected warmth and a sadness to my heart.

Jennifer initially wrote that the divorce decree, along with a couple of depositions, had been sent to the judge. It was just a question of time before his office returned the signed copy. She would forward the filed copy when it became available. At that moment, I realized my life with Jennifer had reached its end.

The second topic Jennifer mentioned was that she was sorry. She understood how awkward her anxiety was for our marriage. She had never meant to hurt me. She agreed that parting was the answer. While this brought a sense of emptiness to her heart, she did convey her excitement as to what the future would hold. I sensed a few tears forming in my eyes.

To clarify her anxiety issues, she wrote that she had visited her physician. During the course of her exam, she noted the situations where anxiety had been problematic in the marriage. She was struggling with why these situations kept recurring. However, sometimes complex problems have simple answers.

Based on this background information, her doctor performed an extensive examination. He eventually attributed her anxiety to a physiological basis. She had developed some type of hormonal deficiency. The doctor concluded that hormonal injections along with a small dose of an anti-anxiety pill would significantly reduce any anxiety. I was astonished at this news. If I had known, maybe we would not have taken separate paths.

My heart sank further upon reading the final paragraph. Her new boyfriend had proposed. Jennifer quickly accepted. They had visited the doctor concerning their desire to have a baby. Jennifer clarified that a baby would bring her closer to her fiancé. A child would further reduce any anxiety she possessed. Her last sentence mentioned that Jenny and Dalton were well, and they wanted to say hello. While I longed to see Jennifer happy, my heart ached at this news. It was shocking that our problems may have required such a simple answer.

I could no longer hold back the tears. I had the same emptiness in my stomach that developed when my first girlfriend broke up with me many years ago. No feeling I experienced was more difficult to manage than dealing with that kind of heartbreak. I prayed for God's compassion and comfort.

Jennifer concluded her letter by wishing me well for my future. She wanted me to find comfort in discovering myself. After another prayer, my emotions started to turn. While my heart was empty, I believed God would provide all the answers with my journey to Faith. At that exact moment, I saw a clear rainbow to the east as I resumed my journey out of Little Rock.

Surprise Phone Call

It did not take my attitude long to change from emptiness to a fullness that can only be attributed to hope and faith. I always saw a glass filled halfway as a glass half full rather than half empty. There was always optimism in my heart and spirit. That attitude would continue all the way toward Memphis.

I began to relive memories of only a few days ago. I had traversed this same stretch of highway. I wondered how Charles and Sarah were dealing with life's chaos. I also thought about how Faith was handling the death of her childhood sweetheart, Gabe. Finally, I remembered the shooting stars that made a lasting impression on my spirit.

I thought of an interpretation for those falling celestial bodies. The first I saw came around the time Gabe had passed away. Clearly, this bright star seemed to be a sign from God as to that event. The second star was more troubling. It seemed to dim before it faded completely from the sky. Maybe this sign was a prelude of the accident where Faith had died. However, she did not really die. My efforts revived her. As a result, that bright light had yet to fade from the earth.

I started listening to my valued Christian music. I once again started singing.

Conditions had improved substantially from Little Rock. No more rain and storms occupied the night sky. I could see the moon greeting me in the distance. It was as if it beckoned me forward on my journey.

Soon, I would arrive in Memphis.

Upon seeing the bridges and the city skyline in the twilight, I wanted to stop briefly. I wanted to eat a quick sandwich and drink a juice while walking by the river. These serene and quiet moments did much to soothe my heart. Afterwards, I planned to return to driving. My goal remained to talk and visit with Faith. I would take whatever time God would allow me with her. I know God had a plan for both of us. My gut instinct compelled the thought that we would be in this life together.

I arrived in Memphis as my heart was filling with excitement. Soon, I would be visiting the very woman whose life I saved a few days before. I would also be able to talk to Charles and Sarah. It would feel great to see them again. I finally pulled into the lot next to the Mississippi River, parked, and shut off my engine. I took a few deep breaths. I made a plain sandwich and grabbed a juice from the cooler. It was then that I would take another walk that would ultimately change my life.

I was deep in thought as I ate and walked. I glanced at the river with its foreboding vastness next to me. I thought about how good it would feel to have someone like Faith to take that walk with me. I finished my snack and juice and stared at the lights from the city as well as the ripples of the water. Surprisingly, I was not prepared for what was about to happen.

I felt history was repeating itself when my phone started ringing from my pocket. As I pulled it from my pocket, I noticed that the call was restricted. I had no way of knowing who this might be. On the other hand, there were a few people who would call me at that time. I suspected that the call originated in some fashion from the hospital. I immediately prayed that it was not bad news. A relapse of Faith's condition would be devastating for my heart. I answered the call with a simple hello. I followed by asking who was calling.

I heard the soft, familiar voice of a female. She asked me if my name was Frank. I answered affirmatively. She finally identified herself. As I was walking by the river, I stopped abruptly. I was stunned at the words that followed. She said her name was Faith Jennings.

Following that immediate and intense revelation, I went into shock. Silence permeated the line. I could no longer speak. Soon, I heard her question me by saying hello again. She inquired if I was still on the line.

Gathering my composure, I told her I was surprised she would call. I suspected it might be someone from the hospital. I had developed a budding friendship with her parents. I would have never anticipated that she would be calling in her condition. I told her I was indeed Frank. I made it clear it was an absolute privilege to be speaking to her. While I could now speak, I felt as nervous as a young boy talking to a beautiful cheerleader for the first time. I became captivated by the southern charm in her voice. I began to visualize the face I had seen in the mist. Nonetheless, I wondered why she would even call.

She began by stating there were a few things she needed to tell me. The first comment she made was that she wanted to thank me. She was informed by her father that a gentleman had saved her life. Her father did not yet know who he was. When the older paramedic checked her condition a few days later, Faith wondered if he knew. He quickly told her my name and provided my cell phone number. Additionally, and oddly enough, she felt she had a dream about me. Hence, she felt inspired to call.

As I gathered my nerves, I told her it was all right. I did what faith and compassion demanded. I could not let her die in that manner. I felt her life was just too valuable.

I interjected that I was even on my way to see her. I wanted to know more about her. I mentioned that I had experienced occurrences that led me to her. God had provided the path for this amazing journey. He had reasons and a plan for the events bringing us together.

Unfortunately, Faith indicated a second reason for the call. She explicitly stated that she could not see me. Tragedies in her life had riddled her heart with serious depression and confusion. Although she appreciated my thoughts and concerns, she had a battle to wage. She needed to journey beyond her tragedies. With her experiences with loss in her life, she could not afford another attachment only to be whisked away by the hand of fate. She said she was sorry.

I told her I understood. Yet as a lawyer, I wanted an opportunity to convey my arguments for seeing and getting to know her. I tried to inject inspiration into my tone. I told her succinctly that pain is an essential part of living. No one can fear pain. Not taking the good with the bad would certainly reduce the quality of one's life. One appreciates the good experiences when having to undergo the bad moments.

She had experienced so much bad. I tried to convince her that only good was destined to follow. I concluded my thoughts by saying that older people have regrets concerning things they did not do rather than those they did.

While attentive to this argument, Faith maintained her distance in allowing me to touch her heart. She was reluctant to get to know me. However, I had one fleeting counteroffer. I wanted her to spend the next few days learning about me. I was confident I was not going anywhere. After that time, if she felt the same, I would continue down God's chosen path without her. I would leave her and her family alone to confront the jaws of fate that had bitten them severely. She would always be in my prayers.

Faith hesitated. Seeing some truth and inspiration in my message, she reluctantly agreed to see me when I arrived in Nashville. She said she owed it to God to meet with the valiant knight who had rescued the damsel in distress. After these encouraging words, the phone line went silent.

I returned to my truck. At that moment, my perception was that my glass remained half full. I felt sure that I would have a significant challenge when I arrived at the hospital. Still, God's mighty hand had delivered me to this point. I had to see events to their conclusion. My faith would not have it any other way. At that moment, I saw the lights of Memphis in my side mirrors. God and Faith awaited my arrival at the end of the road.

CHAPTER 14

A Little Help Convincing Faith

Finding St. John's and Faith

With the somber moments one experiences in life, this adversity should never be the end. After sadness, there should always be a new beginning. God will provide blessings if we expect and prepare for them. All this outlook requires is hope and faith. I had a difficult challenge in conveying this mindset to Faith.

Driving away from Memphis, I had to formulate words to convince Faith that our friendship was important to her recovery. She needed my inspirational crane to extract her from her huge abyss of depression. I felt God would provide all the tools to achieve this objective. After all, He had directed me this far.

The wheels of time kept rolling as I approached the halfway point to Nashville. I decided to quickly stop in Jackson, Tennessee, for some fuel. As an inspiration, I decided to search through a list of bible verses I carry with me. My grandmother gave me this list a few weeks before she died. It was imperative that I discover the right one to convey to Faith.

As I was filling the tank, one verse stood out. The verse seemed to catch the essence of what Faith was experiencing. I read the verse a couple of times:

Your life will be brighter than noonday. Even darkness will be bright as morning. Having hope will give you courage. You will be protected and will rest in safety. You will lie down unafraid, and many will look to you for help.
Job 11:17-19.

With my thought process, I was even convincing myself that I was the best thing that could happen in Faith's life at this time.

I returned to the freeway. I also mentally composed a list of questions centering on the unexplained events in my life. Would she know Miri? Did she recognize the old woman at the cross if I described her? Why was God pulling my heart in her direction? I was hopeful she would assist me in completing the divinely inspired masterpiece God wanted me to finish.

At a steady speed with little traffic, I quickly arrived in Nashville. I stopped briefly at a truck stop near the Grand Ole Opry. I knew that Faith's hospital was close. I took a few minutes to revive and compose myself. I knew I had to be in top form to provide a convincing argument as to why Faith should continue to see me.

I easily found St. John's Memorial Hospital after driving a short distance. It was much larger than portrayed on the billboard. I also noticed the path running down a short hill from the rear of the building. I saw several feet of the path. I was able to discern a few benches with crosses in the back. Trees eventually obstructed my view as my eyes continued following the path. I still had a strong feeling I had been in this area before.

Visions of the surreal moments I had experienced filled my thoughts as I approached the hospital entrance. My thoughts became jumbled as I entered. My heart began racing and I sensed my palms getting sweaty. I would finally be meeting one of the most beautiful women I had ever seen.

Once inside the hospital, I observed a circular information center. I noticed a couple of individuals behind the glass enclosure. A young female associate was sitting in front behind a desk. Her name badge revealed her identity as Anna. Another tall man was walking toward the rear with papers in his hand. Anna greeted me when I approached. She asked how she could help me. Her demeanor was sweet and compassionate. I suppose this attitude should be expected of an associate in her position.

I smiled and introduced myself. I inquired if Faith Jennings was a patient. I also needed to know her room number. After checking on her computer, she acknowledged that Faith was, in fact, a patient. She had been moved from intensive care a few days earlier. Anna graciously provided directions to the elevator to the floor of her room: room 316.

I expressed my appreciation. However, she interjected that visiting hours would end in forty-five minutes. My final inquiry was the location of a gift shop. She gladly pointed me in that direction. From that moment, I had no time to waste.

After purchasing a couple of items from the gift shop, I quickly arrived at the third floor. I had purchased a card, a Get-Well balloon, and a stuffed little dog. I was hoping the initial greeting would impress Faith. I quickly arrived at the nurse's station. A nurse provided directions to Faith's room. Sadly, she added that visiting hours would conclude in thirty minutes.

I took a few deep breaths as I walked in Faith's direction. Nearing the room, I saw Charles exit. Sarah was following him. In a raised voice, I called out their names. Immediately, they turned in my direction.

Upon recognizing me, they quickly approached where I was standing. Tears started flowing from all of us as we embraced outside Faith's room. Charles expressed his thanks for my presence. Most importantly, he found out I was the good Samaritan who saved Faith's life. Sarah also gave me a kind hug. I asked one simple question: Could I see Faith before visiting hours ended?

Charles directed me to the door. He and Sarah excused themselves. They were heading for the restroom when I got their attention. Charles's last words were to thank me for coming. My appearance meant a lot to him and Sarah. Finally, he wanted me to tell Faith that we loved her. I agreed. They turned and walked away.

The moment of truth had arrived. I softly knocked on Faith's door. She provided approval for me to enter. As I walked in, I identified myself. Our eyes met. There was an incredible electricity I had never experienced. I genuinely felt that I was looking into the eyes of an angel. No words can even approach the sensation I was feeling.

She thanked me for the gifts and the card. Like her parents, she appreciated my visit. It was important for her to meet the man who saved her. She would always remember. After that expression, our conversation took on a more ominous tone.

Tears were forming in Faith's eyes. She whispered that she was having a tough time dealing with depression. The loss of Gabe pushed her emotions off the highest mountain peak. She claimed that she may never recover. After this meeting, she could not see me anymore. She could not handle another loss. A torrent of tears fell down her cheeks. She could no longer speak.

As I did not have much time, I explained that God's hand had directed me to her. I mentioned the dreams with a mysterious woman, the older woman at the cross, my journey to Nashville, and finally saving her life. I told Faith I had one request: please listen to my inspirational arguments before pushing me over a shared emotional cliff. All I asked was that she understand and provide me with a little time.

I sensed my attempts at persuasion were falling on deaf ears. Her sobbing became more intense. I tried to comfort her. Initially, no words seemed to be working. However, I said a little prayer. I reached deep into my inspirational knowledge provided by my grandparents. It was this effort I sensed was changing Faith's emotional tide.

In a soft voice, I tried desperately to calm her. My first words were that God and faith would provide for her needs. God surely would take care of her. While Faith seemed to respond to this oratory, she continued crying.

I held one of her hands as I continued. I added that when God put hearts inside us, we should understand that there would be a chance they would break. Despite that, He understands what we feel. I emphasized that, through faith, God will take the pain away. Through prayer and understanding, all battles can be successfully waged and won through faith and God's understanding.

While she continued crying, the sobs appeared to lessen. I believe I then made a comment that struck a nerve with Faith. I said that everyone, including myself, has wounds that may never heal. But it is up to everyone to work together to bind those wounds. I also mentioned the sunrise I had seen during my first run out west. As I described the elongated flame coming from the horizon, her eyes gazed into mine. I remembered I had taken a solitary photograph using my cell phone. At that moment, I showed this image to Faith. The beauty in our world is amazing. I emphasized my belief that I had sensed God's very presence. He had helped me save her. She could return to her feet, have faith, and God would help her be better and stronger than she ever was. While not totally sure of what Faith might be thinking, I felt I had made progress.

She had stopped crying completely.

After a brief silence, she said that I reminded her of Gabe. When she was being bullied, he refused to let the other classmates push her down. His tone was uplifting and inspirational. She surprisingly mentioned that he was like an angel God sent just for her. I almost saw a smile come over the soft fullness of her lips. I made the same effort to try to lift her spirits in a time of profound sadness.

Finally, I told her of the inspirational verse my grandmother's list had provided. I emphasized the last words. Individuals in her life genuinely needed her. They would be lost without her. I realized my words had finally made an impact as she stared at me while tightly squeezing my hand. I felt God had helped me accomplish His purpose.

With a serious look on her face, Faith agreed to visit with me the next day. A bell sounded, indicating that visiting hours were nearly over. I had little time remaining. I added one last comment: Sometimes you have to be lost and without hope to really be found. I added that I encountered her parents, and they wanted me to convey that we loved her. I started to walk away. I said it was a pleasure. I would come by as soon as visiting hours recommenced the next day. She smiled. Yet the words she concluded with were shockingly familiar. She wanted me to review a bible verse: Isaiah 41:10. While I was surprised, I nodded affirmatively as I exited the room. Visiting hours had ended.

Joining Miri and Faith in the Mist

The bible verse Faith cited sounded familiar. Why did Isaiah 41:10 hit a nerve in my heart? When was the last time I reviewed it? Suddenly, I perceived the answer.

This verse was the same verse I quoted to Faith when I first met this angelic woman in the mist. Isaiah 41:10 expounds on the feeling that God will help and strengthen any person. This person had nothing to fear if he had a sincere belief in God. My words were having an impact.

Hopefully, this impact would continue as I attempted to win the key to the lock on Faith's heart.

I exited the building and proceeded to my truck. I got in, started the engine, and returned to the truck stop I patronized when I first arrived. I was exhausted from the long and emotional day.

I turned on some soft classical music. I drank some bottled water from my cooler as I stared outside my window. I observed other trucks coming and going. What was Faith thinking? In a romantic way, would God provide me a chance to win Faith's broken heart? I finally set my alarm. Eventually, the exhaustion overtook my body. After lying down, I immediately fell into a deep sleep.

There was a darkness that slowly turned into light. I found myself walking again. There was the same mist surrounding me. However, I sensed a warmth within the mist that I had never experienced. I hoped to see Miri once more. If I did see her, maybe she would supply answers to questions remaining unanswered.

I slowly navigated along the path. Because of my familiarity with this path, my steps quickened as I searched for the white gazebo. I had yet to hear the thunder or see the lightning that had shortened prior visits to this mist.

There was a peace to this moment I had never felt. In my mind, I questioned what this meant.

Eventually, I was able to discern the silhouette of the gazebo embedded in the mist. I slowly began to detect two individuals seated inside. I recognized that they were female after seeing their long hair and particular disposition as I approached. However, I was not prepared for what I ultimately saw.

The two women seated looked identical. They had the same hairstyle, the same facial features, and the same body type. It was as if the one was looking at herself in a mirror. The only distinguishing characteristic was that the woman on the right had healing abrasions in a few spots on her head. I was certainly puzzled by what I had perceived.

They were talking and holding hands when I reached the gazebo doorway. I noticed a few tears on the face of the woman on the right. While the woman on the left had no distinct dialect, there was a unique southern accent to the conversation from the woman she was facing.

This observation led me to one conclusion. Miri was on the left while Faith was seated on the right. Yet what did this mean?

Once they saw me, they stopped talking. Both women gazed into my eyes. I questioned them as to what was happening. They gave me the impression that they knew each other. Who exactly were they? After a brief period of silence, the woman on the right responded. She identified herself as Faith. What Faith stated next left me speechless. I finally had the answer to a paramount question plaguing me during my adventures.

Faith introduced me to Miri: Miranda Abigail Jennings. Faith mentioned Miri was a nickname she gave to her deceased twin when she was younger. Miri interjected that she liked it because the name was short and sweet. Miri added that in some way, she was sent to try to help Faith through her troubled times. Unfortunately, she could only make her presence felt in the mist. She felt Faith required my friendship at this time in her life. I could open doors that Faith's heartache was trying to close. Miri plainly said that I could be the inspiration essential to reestablish meaning to Faith's unstable life. This meaning had faded with the tragic events in Faith's recent past.

However, Miri was stuck. She was having a difficult time convincing Faith.

The mental chasm Faith had slipped through was so deep that Miri questioned what help she could be. She needed my help. One person may not be able to move the mountain. However, many sources providing continuous inspirational fortitude will provide the dynamite to blow that mountain of depression away.

I finally understood. All my travails pointed to how I needed to restore Faith's mental health. Miri and her parents had experienced little success in their efforts. Miri had hope that I would be the answer. While this effort seemed formidable, I conveyed to Miri and Faith that I was ready to confront this challenge.

Miri mentioned the past. Specifically, she spoke of the previous encounters in the mist. She needed me. A cloud of darkness appeared over Faith's head and was affecting her very being. In some fashion, Miri felt that with my faith and hope, I would provide Faith with the inspirational cure. That fact was why Miri felt she needed to communicate with me. I knew I needed to help Faith find the answers. I thought about how I left Jennifer. I definitely could not leave Faith the same way after saving her life.

Miri stated she had to leave. She indicated that it was prudent for me to stay there with Faith. With my power of persuasion, I needed to keep inspiring. Faith needed this repeated encouragement. This continual effort would provide the crutch to overcome her sadness.

As Miri walked in the distance, I asked Faith if she wanted to walk. She agreed. We quickly found ourselves on the bench where we sat after I first met her in the mist. The sound of the bubbling brook captivated our senses. The birds were chirping in the distance. Finally, a full moon appeared above us reflecting against the ripples in this stream. The ambience seemed appropriate for providing the curative inspiration.

Faith started the conversation. I could tell her emotions were gradually bubbling to the surface. She said how much she loved her grandmother. Eliza Faith meant everything to her. While her parents were working, her grandmother took care of her needs and inspired her heart. When she found her grandmother dead, it felt like a bolt of lightning burned her very soul. Yet counseling helped to revitalize that spirit.

As Faith was recovering from that trauma, she met Gabe. His response to her bullies won her heart. At that moment, Faith fell in love with this young man as he protected her and guarded her soul. Surprisingly, Faith claimed that I possessed the same protective attribute. Faith was attracted to me as well because of it.

When Faith continued, tears were starting to form and fall from her eyes. She mentioned the miscarriage. She and Gabe had prepared for this baby.

Their hearts were excited at the prospect of this new little emergence into their lives. It was hard to understand why the miscarriage happened. I reached for her hands and took them in mine. I told her my heart ached with sadness.

Faith then mentioned Baby Gabe. That baby boy was the greatest gift God ever provided. Her life was complete after his birth. She had the ideal man with a perfect family. Why did it have to end? Like a water faucet, her tears became incessant streams down both cheeks. She slowly lost her emotional composure.

I reached into my pocket. I reviewed my grandmother's inspirational list of verses. Before I had the chance to read an appropriate verse, Faith asked what this paper was. I explained the bible verses and how my grandmother had written the list. I told Faith how close we were. While her tears remained steady, the magnitude of her crying did not increase. The closeness to our grandmothers was another aspect we shared.

I finally found a verse befitting the mournful situation we found ourselves.

This verse states:

Blessed are those who mourn, for they will be comforted. Matthew 5:4.

I boldly told Faith that this verse is in no way ambiguous. God definitively will provide comfort during adversity. All we have to do is ask.

I tried to distract Faith to quell her rising sobs. I noticed two necklaces she was wearing. I remembered seeing those after the accident. One was a cross; the other was a locket. I asked Faith about the locket. Since I had frequently encountered surprises during my adventures, I could not have anticipated what would happen next.

Faith revealed that the locket was a gift from Gabe. Inside the locket, she had placed a small photograph of her grandmother. At this point, her tears had ceased. She opened the locket so I could see the image. I was shocked at the sight of the image. The picture was the same older woman I had seen at the cross, and when I visited my grandparents' graves. I was speechless.

A chill wind began blowing in our faces. I felt a look of consternation on my face. Faith asked me if I was fine. I briefly told her about the similarities between the old woman at the cross and the one in the locket. I may have seen the spirit of her grandmother. After this statement, there was a loud clap of thunder. Immediately, Faith disappeared, and everything turned to darkness.

CHAPTER 15

The Challenge to Convince Faith

The Relevance of the Locket

The sound of the ambulance siren reverberated throughout the cab of my truck. The noise shook me out of my deep slumber. It was almost as if the ambulance was right outside my window. I took a few deep breaths to gather my composure.

Since my alarm was due to ring shortly, I could not go back to sleep. My thoughts focused solely on Faith. I had learned a great deal from her; first, by visiting her in her room, preceded by the first encounter in the mist, followed by the second meeting in the mist with Miri. I had one major question in my mind. Were my efforts having an impact on Faith's depression?

This main question preoccupied my mind as I prepared to visit Faith again. A fear started to enter my heart. What if I exhausted the inspirational tasks I had at my disposal? What if Faith continued to be emotional and unresponsive to my efforts? More urgent was the question whether she would become suicidal. After more deep breaths, I silently prayed God would furnish the answers. I felt His divine path would not lead me to failure.

After I showered, I got dressed. At that moment, I thought about the locket. I thought about Faith's grandmother. I remembered her presence at the cross.

The first time I saw her, she pointed east. This gesture represented her effort to compel me to travel in Faith's direction. I never could have predicted I would eventually save her granddaughter's life.

When I was driving toward Nashville, this same image reappeared at the cross. She stretched out her arms as if she were beckoning me for a hug. Maybe this was a sign of endearment since I was heading in Faith's direction. She appeared thankful for the effort I was making. Faith did say that her grandmother meant everything to her.

The final time I saw this image was at my grandparents' graves. Not only did this older woman appear to seek a hug, but she also mouthed inaudible words.

These words seemed to convey thanks for some reason. Since I had recently saved Faith's life, clearly her grandmother had reason to thank me for my life-saving efforts. I could think of no other plausible answer. In some way, her grandmother would be critical in devising a solution to alleviate Faith's depression. Unquestionably, I had to factor in her grandmother to produce the inspirational solution I was desperate for.

When I was finally ready, I had a chocolate Bismarck with a small coffee. While my thoughts centered on Faith, my anxiety started to increase.

In a few days, I would have to resume my truck driving career. I was optimistic I would resolve Faith's depression before then. I needed to cast away any doubt. I had to continue to perceive the glass as half-full. Ending with that thought, I returned to the hospital.

Continued Quest to Inspire Faith

The stress of my continued quest began to increase astronomically. Not only was the stress of my career creeping into my mind, but I also began to have doubts concerning the emotional progress I was making with Faith. While I was optimistic, it was hard not to get discouraged with all the pain Faith endured. I continued to believe God was directing me along His path. Like a fairy tale, I would find light at the end of the tunnel I had traveled.

Upon my return to the hospital, I proceeded to the entrance. I quickly passed the information desk. I smiled and nodded at

Anna. She stated that only a couple of hours were allowed for me to visit in the morning.

Unfortunately, Faith would be undergoing an intensive psychological evaluation in the afternoon. Sadly, I would not have much time to spend during the day lifting her spirits. However, I turned to prayer to ask God for the most productive use of my time.

When I arrived at Faith's room, I discovered the door was closed. After a knock, I opened the door and entered. Faith had her eyes closed. She had a very worn and haggard look on her face. This sight brought tears to my eyes.

The depressed feeling was overwhelming. For the first time, I was wondering if my efforts were futile. Was the depression instilled by Faith's tragedies too much for my inspirational effort to overcome?

I reached for Faith's hands. I held them firmly and said a quiet prayer. She must have sensed my presence since her eyes started to open. At that moment, tears began streaming from her eyes. I felt at a loss to understand. Was my presence responsible for her tears?

Why was Faith crying? I tried to calm her. In a quiet voice, I told her everything would be fine. I was there for her. I was not going to leave her.

She answered by whispering that everyone she loves leaves her. Last night, Miri had left her in the mist. Furthermore, with the loud clap of thunder, I was gone. The list seemed to grow in her mind. Even her parents had not yet stopped to visit. She finally asked a simple question: "How can I regain my spirit when everyone disappears?"

I tried to convey that I understood the way she felt. As I squeezed her hands, I told her boldly that I was here with her now. Yet she inquired how long my presence would last. I felt I was fighting a losing battle.

I did not lose sight of my determination. I asked her if she would enjoy taking a walk with me. I mentioned the path behind the hospital. It was a beautiful and bright day. In my mind, I felt this walk was exactly what Faith needed. While Faith initially was hesitant, she finally agreed.

To begin our trek, a nurse brought Faith a wheelchair. It was hospital policy to follow this protocol. I told Faith I would enjoy pushing her down the path. We would have plenty of time to converse. This effort at communication hopefully would have a purging effect on her sadness. I was willing to try anything. Seeing Faith eventually smile again would be worth the effort.

We began our slow journey down the path. It was as if I had traveled this way many times. We observed the benches with the crosses. The bubbling brook echoed in the distance. Birds were happily chirping in the sunshine. Faith was silent. She seemed deep in thought as we approached the gazebo.

Faith asked if we could stop for a minute. I undoubtedly concurred. At that moment, Faith commenced a long oration. I felt this journey was starting to produce a cathartic effect. I allowed her uninterrupted expressiveness to continue.

Faith spoke of her grandmother. They truly loved and cared for each other. She had experienced some faint images of herself in her dreams. However, these images were brief. While her grandmother appeared to talk, she could not hear any audible sound from her lips. Just as quickly as the image materialized, it disappeared into an unimaginable darkness. She asked me what this meant.

Yet, not providing time for a response, Faith continued to dominate the conversation. Her voice started to crack as she mentioned she had navigated this path many times. The first time was to go outside and contemplate after her miscarriage. She was brought to St. John's too late to save her pregnancy. While that moment was hard, Gabe had been there to comfort her. She stated she felt the same comfort with my presence.

Faith began lightly sobbing as she recalled Baby Gabe. When he became ill, he was brought to the cancer unit for treatment. Faith pointed up the hill at the facility. No words could describe the heartache caused by the baby's condition. None of the treatments available (radiation and chemotherapy) made any difference.

Faith reminisced on her brief time with Baby Gabe. This little blessing created more joy than she and Gabe could have ever imagined. He was born healthy with a sparkle in his eyes. He was a reflection of his father. Her life seemed perfect after his birth.

Baby Gabe at birth weighed over eight pounds. He always appeared to be a fast learner. He was babbling earlier than normal. Faith was impressed when he learned the words "momma" and "dadda" before he turned one. He also learned how to walk four months before his first birthday. She and Gabe radiated pride at the presence of this child.

Faith stayed at home with the baby while Gabe worked. Faith recalled how they would go outside and play together. Baby Gabe had a red ball the size of a basketball. He loved tossing this ball with his parents. Moreover, Faith enjoyed their walks along a nearby scenic river path when she had the opportunity. She loved every precious moment with her son.

It was during one of these trips to the river that a seemingly insignificant event would lead to the ominous health discovery. On this trip, Faith began playfully chasing Baby Gabe along the path when Baby Gabe stumbled. While not seriously hurt, he had a little gash on his knee. He also skinned his elbows and legs mildly. While Baby Gabe was crying, Faith told him she was sorry. She would look after him and promised he would be fine. She immediately took him home to treat his wounds.

A short time later, Faith noticed the wounds were not healing. Moreover, other symptoms gradually appeared. Baby Gabe was not as playful. He became lethargic and spent hours in his room. When Faith asked him if he was okay, he grimaced like he was feeling pain.

Thereafter, his appetite disappeared. He stopped eating. He began losing weight. Alarmed at these events, Faith asked Gabe to drive them to the hospital. The doctors would finally diagnose the reason: acute leukemia.

Faith felt she was somehow responsible for Baby Gabe's condition. She emphasized that she was the one who was chasing Baby Gabe along the path. She caused him to trip. She was responsible for his wounds. She was responsible for his deteriorating health. She became speechless as her sobbing amplified with her emotions. After several minutes, her sobbing lessened.

Before I could speak, Faith resumed her monologue. She stated how much she was missing Gabe. His persistent attitude to protect her was the most attractive quality about him. The way he smiled at her emitted a quality of love and compassion she had never seen. She knew almost immediately that Gabe was the man for her.

They became inseparable before they graduated. They sat together in classes. They ate lunch together. After school, they even did their homework together before eating supper. Faith did little to hide the fact that she believed they were destined to spend their lives together.

Tears reappeared in Faith's eyes. She mentioned the many times she baked her grandmother's butterscotch cookies. Faith would bring these cookies to school to share with Gabe. He would always exclaim that no one in the world made better cookies. The glow from Gabe's eyes showed his sincerity when he spoke.

Not only did Gabe stop the bullying Faith experienced, but his tone also frequently diverted her from any pit of sadness she stumbled upon. Gabe offered this support consistently after the miscarriage. While she knew he was also hurting, he was an absolute pillar of strength. As the frequency of her tears increased, Faith exclaimed that she was never cognizant of how much she leaned on Gabe when times were bad.

Even though Faith felt the need for counseling, Gabe's strength was always in the background. His love, hope, and encouragement filled her heart like the wind blowing the sail of a stalled ship. She journeyed forward knowing Gabe would be at her side. His encouragement led to the renewed attempt to have a baby.

This attempt paid off with the birth of Baby Gabe. Gabe spent his free time after work with Faith and the baby. Faith recalled times Gabe and his son would be sitting on the couch. When Gabe was not reading a storybook with pictures (Baby Gabe loved pictures!), he would recite bible verses to his son. Baby Gabe responded with the cutest smiles. It was obvious Faith loved the simple life with her simple family.

This simple life came crashing down like a huge rock thrown through a plate glass window. When Faith discovered Gabe had a brain tumor, her first reaction was shock. Gabe could not be that ill. This sentiment progressed to one of profound heartache at her impending loss. The current moment on the path captured the sorrow of Gabe's fight when both Faith and I looked toward the cancer facility. How could Gabe be that ill so young? Faith felt she was losing the strength she relied on to live and thrive.

After a nurse came by to indicate our time together was almost at its end, Faith started sobbing again. She whispered that she had not been able to attend Gabe's funeral. A drunk driver hit her car as she was attempting to make final arrangements. When her light turned to darkness, she thought she had died. In her mind, maybe her death would have been an unexpected blessing.

While a part of Faith was discouraged, she met me in the mist. She was contemplating why she should even live. She even had suicidal thoughts. My eyes, my voice, and my heart gave her courage to try to live again. Sitting with me on the bench, my inspiration helped lift her depression to an extent. When she was alone, her suicidal thoughts would return. She felt she bore the responsibility for her losses.

I knelt and held her. Tears were running down my cheeks. After a brief moment, she pushed me away. I did not understand. Faith would provide a shocking blow to my heart.

With all the pain and depression, Faith adamantly conveyed through her tears that she could never see me again. With the pain and emptiness that she had illustrated, her heart couldn't withstand any more depression. She would be undergoing an extensive evaluation during the next few days. She would not be able to have visitors. Faith finally commented that we should leave our relationship as it was. We would remain distant friends. She would remember and appreciate my saving her life.

Before I could speak, Charles and Sarah had finally arrived. Their automobile had a flat tire on the way that took a significant amount of time to repair. Faith greeted them. She emphatically commanded that her parents return her to her room. Charles and Sarah said they were sorry as they began to wheel her away. I was left speechless and in shock. I could not have appreciated the intensity of Faith's mental fragility. I yelled at Faith that I would not be leaving that easily. I would always be there for her. As they disappeared up the hill, my final tearful prayer was to ask God what I could do to help her.

CHAPTER 16

The Search for an Answer

Faith's Impenetrable Wall

My heart ached as I reversed my route along the hospital path. I felt as frustrated and helpless as any time in my life. I tried every remedy I knew to show Faith her life would only get better. These attempts included reciting bible verses to kind spirited words. However, these attempts went awry. Faith was successfully shielding me from her heart.

I could not say I blamed her. Her tragedies had created a significant wound to her emotions. She truly felt alone. The emotional intensity increased when there was no one around. I understood how she might feel responsible and that I would leave too. After all, I did leave Jennifer.

I began to have flashbacks to Jennifer's anxiety attacks. I never experienced that type of behavior. I did not realize how I could even help her. I thought the only alternative was to leave. However, I sternly refused to leave Faith. I had to develop a final plan to destroy the emotional wall Faith had constructed around herself. I questioned my own mental stability if I ceased my efforts. I sensed God was guiding me in this endeavor.

As I was passing the information center, Anna stopped me. She stated she had important information concerning Faith. I would not be able to see her over the next few days. Her physician ordered an extensive psychological evaluation. The doctor demanded no visitors temporarily in order to accurately record the scope of her depression.

Upon hearing this news, I lost any clue as to what I could do to help. How could I communicate with Faith if I could not see her?

After Anna conveyed this information, I believe she sensed my frustration. To help alleviate this emotion, she asked me for my cell phone number. She wanted to call me at any change in Faith's condition. I also thought she noticed the tears starting to fall down my cheeks. I thanked Anna for her efforts and concern. She smiled and nodded as I exited the hospital.

I remained at a loss as to what to do. My time on leave would end before I had accomplished my objective. I had to formulate one last plan. I had no idea where to start. I had intertwined my faith and inspiration with Faith's life. What could I do to firmly plant Faith's feet back on the ground? Signs from God had brought me to this point. I remained convinced His guiding hand would supply the answer.

Upon returning to my truck, I began to contemplate my agenda. Time would pass, and I would not be able to comfort Faith. I had to devise a course of action with an immediate effect. Was there really something else I could do? Was there another course of action I could take? I prayed that Faith's depression did not worsen. At that moment, I had a piercing thought that raised my anxiety.

I had thoughts about Ms. Santos. I remembered being informed of her suicide. I experienced shock followed by intense grief. I certainly could not let that happen with Faith. She seemed to have an aura that was angelic, caring, and full of inspiration. I felt that once some time had elapsed from her last tragedy, she would gradually commence a very slow healing process. My last thought was why God would bring me this far only to see Faith kill herself.

I spent the bulk of the afternoon and evening contemplating what to do. I did some laundry and ran a few errands. After a brief dinner, I went for a long walk. All that time, I analyzed how I could at least communicate with Faith. I continued to be in shock at how belligerent she was when I saw her last.

I found a secluded spot at the rear of the truck stop near Faith. Before long, the sun set signaling the end of a trying day. I started listening to a new Christian DVD I had purchased earlier that afternoon. As I sat in the driver's seat, I saw a river in the distance to my right. To my left, I saw the distant skyline of Nashville. Recalling my trips to Groom, Texas, I detected a feeling that in a remote way, Eliza Faith held the key to the completion of my puzzle. I remembered my trips to the cross, Faith's locket, and her dreams concerning her grandmother. Yet what exactly was the answer? I closed my eyes. Soon, I drifted away into another heavy slumber.

Meeting Eliza Faith in the Mist

After what seemed to be a few seconds, darkness again turned to light. I found myself wandering along the path in the mist. Realizing I had seen Miri and Faith the last time I was here, I had no preconceived idea of what to expect this time. I quietly uttered a prayer that God would provide similar light in the darkness prevalent in my real life during this excursion.

I slowly walked by the benches scattered by the stream. Nothing seemed out of the ordinary except for a warm swirling wind encompassing my body. In this reality, sometimes feelings and sounds seemed unusual. However, the chirping of the birds along with the sound of the brook erased any feeling of uneasiness. I had to discern the reason for this visit.

Like my other trips here, I slowly walked down the path to find the gazebo. In my reality, this was the last location where I spoke with Faith. My heart ached at not being able to see and speak to her. I remained at a loss for what action to take to truly assist her mental health.

I found the gazebo well-lit when I arrived. Nonetheless, no one was near it. After walking around the structure, I began to shout. First, I yelled Miri's name. Immediately thereafter, I yelled for Faith. No response. There was an eerie quiet I had yet to experience in this locale. Looking around in all directions, the invading mist saturated the areas around the path.

I left the gazebo and continued walking. I passed a few benches while listening to the birds and the polite bubbling from the creek. A bright light illuminated the crosses at the rear of these benches. However, an indistinct sound in the distance captured my attention. The sound appeared to be coming from a person. I had to investigate.

As I got closer, the sound grew more perceptible. I noticed a bench ahead of me. I slowly detected the sound of a person crying. From the whiteness of her hair, this person appeared to be an older woman. Her sobs were increasing in intensity. In an effort to comfort this woman, I moved to the front of the bench. I reached out my hands for hers. I was startled when she gazed into my eyes. I had seen this woman before.

Upon making eye contact, this woman was the person I observed at the cross and at my grandparents' graves. She was the one who made gestures toward me as well as mouthing what appeared to be words of gratitude. Finally, she was the image I saw in Faith's locket. This woman had to be Faith's grandmother, Eliza Faith.

This older woman erased any doubts when she squeezed my hands and identified herself. She declared herself to be Faith's grandmother. She had been trying to help Faith. However, she had not been able to assist her directly. Faith did not seem completely receptive to her visits. Faith seemed to be anxious when she appeared. Eliza Faith was at a loss as to how to help her granddaughter.

Eliza Faith was very cognizant of the tragedies that uprooted Faith's simple life. She had undertaken a desperate effort to get soothing messages to her. She realized the pain that her sudden death created. She wanted Faith to be aware that she was there to help her circumvent the emotion of her losses. Undoubtedly, she had an unparalleled fondness for Faith.

Because of the difficulty in communicating with her beloved granddaughter, she manifested her appearances at the cross. She had been aware of my first meeting in the mist with Miri. Like Miri, she felt her appearance would stimulate my impulse to help. As a living and breathing person, I would be receptive to the messages she conveyed.

With my problem-solving skills, Eliza Faith had confidence in my ability to provide the messages to Faith.

I asked Eliza Faith why she chose to appear at the cross. She provided a simple response. Through Miri, she had discovered that I had started a truck driving career. She timed her appearance to the exact time I would be arriving in the vicinity. While there was uncertainty in her mind concerning whether I would stop, she did pray that God would provide some sensation for me to pause my driving. Since she knew my faith in God was strong, what better place could she choose to make her presence felt?

As she gazed into my eyes, she conveyed her warm gratitude at my effort to save Faith's life. Faith had so much more life to live. It was not her time. Only good moments would prevail for the rest of her living years. Her joys would multiply while her sorrows would lessen.

Similar to Faith's oratory, Eliza Faith's words continued to flow like water coming from a tap that had been completely opened. She confirmed that she was pointing east to direct me toward Faith. With her second appearance at the cross, she indeed wanted to hug me for heading toward Nashville. Finally, while she could mouth certain words, her communication was limited. She wanted to thank me when I visited my grandparents' graves. She could create no discernible sound. She was, however, able to mouth the words. Her ability to communicate was better with me than corresponding efforts with Faith in her dreams. She thanked God for providing me with the ability to understand.

As tears resumed falling from her tired eyes, Eliza Faith said she was at a loss as to the remedies for Faith's woes. She was also privy to my efforts. She understood these efforts were failing. Faith's depression seemed to grow stronger by the minute. She inquired whether I had any thoughts on how to help her assist her granddaughter.

As I stared into Eliza Faith's eyes, I noticed a locket around her neck. This locket looked identical to the one I saw Faith wearing. Sensing my interest, Eliza Faith removed the locket from her neck. She opened it slowly, revealing a photo of Faith at a much younger age. Faith appeared to be the age of a middle school child. Eliza Faith clarified that the photo was taken a few weeks before she died. She was going to show Faith this locket; however, she died before she had a chance.

Eliza Faith possessed an emotional magnetism I had never seen. Although her current sadness shielded her real personality, I could easily detect her true character by the way she communicated with me. She had a genuine interest in my compassion toward Faith. I felt that she knew in her heart that I could provide a spark for a happier life for Faith. Her mannerisms reminded me a lot of my own grandmother.

As Eliza Faith continued talking about her life with Faith, I listened attentively. She mentioned the moment that she held Faith for the first time. While a little feeble at birth, Faith had a powerful aura emanating from her body. Eliza Faith knew that this baby would receive blessings from God. However, she could not easily articulate how these blessings would reveal themselves.

During her infancy, Charles and Sarah requested Eliza Faith to watch over the baby when they worked. Eliza Faith relished the thought of this request. From the moment Faith was born to the morning of the day her grandmother died, Eliza Faith became an integral part of Faith's life. Eliza Faith possessed many admirable qualities she sought to instill in her only granddaughter.

Eliza Faith would read bible verses regularly to Faith. She would also sing hymns she had learned verbatim from an old Baptist church she attended when she was younger. On warmer nights, she would take Faith outside to look at the moon and the stars. Faith had a glow to her eyes during these moments.

Eliza Faith started to hum one of the hymns she sang to Faith. Faith would always smile at her grandmother when she sang this particular song. Moreover, Faith would always try to sing the words with her grandmother. As she got older, she improved her ability to put the words to the notes. There was never a happier time in Eliza Faith's life. As she was concluding this song, I squeezed her hands while gazing into her eyes. I realized how special this moment had become.

Faith's spirit was also captivated by these moments. She loved her grandmother dearly. A special feeling encompassed her heart whenever she was in the presence of her grandmother. Now it was truly apparent how she could be afflicted with such an incomparable heartache. Being with Eliza Faith made me begin praying in earnest that I could find some solution to this family's woes.

Eventually, the words to the hymn reached their conclusion. Eliza Faith was silent for a few minutes. She renewed her inquiry as to how I might be able to help Faith. Tears began falling down her weary cheeks again. She stated that she felt I was her only hope.

I hesitated. However, I recalled a simple bible verse from Joshua that my grandmother recited to me when I was young. I checked my list and was able to find it. This verse read:

Have I not commanded thee? Be strong and of good courage; be not afraid, neither be thou dismayed; for the Lord thy God is with thee whithersoever thou goest. Joshua 1:9.

I was beginning to realize that I was starting to utilize these recitations to provide my own encouragement and inspiration.

Eliza Faith smiled at me. Although she never vocalized the words, she knew then that God would provide the solution through me, my thoughts, and words. She reached over to grasp her purse, which I saw for the first time on the bench. After a bit of rummaging, she removed a couple of papers from one of its pockets. She exclaimed that these were bible verses that had brought her much inspiration and comfort through her life. She wanted me to have this list. Through God, I would be able to find a way to utilize this information in my quest to help Faith.

I graciously took the list. At the same time, I reassured Eliza Faith that I was mentally constructing a scheme to revive Faith's very life. Unfortunately, I had no time to tell Eliza Faith my ideas. The ominous sound of thunder and vicious strikes of lightning reemerged in the distance. I told Eliza Faith we had to go. However, I told her that I would pray and make every effort to maintain some type of contact.

The thunder started its journey closer. The vivid lightning strikes that were once at a distance were proceeding toward the path. Loud bangs of thunder. More lightning. It was almost frightening for me this time in the mist. I saw Eliza Faith disappear down the path in the distance. One more sound of thunder and the light once again turned dark.

CHAPTER 17

The Final Plan to Help Faith

The Origin of the Note

The sound of heavy rain created the ominous start to what appeared to be a dreary day. My lone thought and prayer this morning was how I would ultimately be able to assist Faith. While I could not see her, I was still determined to communicate with her. I could not stand Faith slipping further into a bottomless pit of depression.

My thoughts for a plan began to take shape early this particular morning when I experienced a series of distractions. I quickly went inside the truck stop to shower, get dressed, and purchase a cup of coffee. Upon returning to my truck, my phone alerted me to an incoming text message. This first distraction was a text message from Sunshine Logistics.

Sunshine informed me of the next time and location of my next freight pickup and delivery. The text had been sent by my driver manager, Thomas. I needed to resume driving later the next evening to begin hauling a load from Albuquerque, New Mexico. Ironically, the delivery location would return me to Nashville. I would be hauling spare parts for a wide array of musical instruments. While this text was sooner than I had anticipated, I sincerely felt that I could utilize this information to my advantage.

Shortly after this text, I experienced another distraction. My phone started ringing from an unexpected call. In my haste to respond, I failed to check my caller ID. The voice on the other end sounded very familiar. It was Anna.

Anna said she had some very important information. The primary physician intended to release Faith to her parents the next evening. The doctor would complete his psychological analysis of Faith's depression prior to her discharge. Upon discharge, her parents were free to take her from the hospital. She would then be able to have personal contact with family and friends. Anna felt this news was important for me to hear.

I thanked Anna for this relevant information. However, I sadly advised her that my trucking career dictated that I needed to leave the area tomorrow evening. By departing at that time, I felt I would be restricted in the means at my disposal to help Faith. Still, Anna made a suggestion which almost made me gasp.

God provides uncomplicated tasks to enable one to put together complex answers to gripping questions. Anna recommended that I simply write a note expressing my thoughts and feelings. She would have the ability to personally deliver this note to Faith. Furthermore, this note should consist of the information needed to maintain contact.

While Faith was free to accept or reject this information, once her depression improved, she would have this information handy when she was ready for contact. Anna stated she supported my efforts and wanted to help. As I do not believe events happen coincidentally, I told Anna I would indeed write a lengthy note to Faith with the inspiration and support she needed.

I once again thanked Anna for the call. More importantly, I was appreciative of the information and the suggestion. God was directing me down the final path to create the masterpiece He yearned for. All the signs were pointing in the same direction. I would find a way to assist Faith. My heart began to fill with optimism.

The Contents of the Note

The solitary call coupled with the presence of Eliza Faith in the mist helped to firmly implant in my mind an outline of a plan to help Faith. My first step was to compose a note. This note would consist of three parts. In my judgment, each part alone would be insufficient to modify Faith's depression. However, taken as a whole, these parts would act as a sledgehammer, forcing Faith's wall of depression to crumble.

As the heavy rain continued, I stayed inside my cab composing Faith's note. Reliving my time in the mist with her special grandmother, I could not even bear to see either woman cry again. Faith's grandmother would serve as the inspiration for my continued efforts. I also did not want Faith's soul tormented any longer. As God had me in His plans, I no longer had any doubt He would let my efforts fail.

My first point was to tell Faith about my visit in the mist with her beloved grandmother. I wrote in the note how Eliza Faith had visited her in her dreams. Eliza Faith wanted to comfort her; however, Faith experienced anxiety when she observed this image. This uncertainty in perception created a barrier to Eliza Faith's effective presence and communication. I tried to inform Faith that I would make every effort to place her in situations where she could visit with her grandmother. In time, the efforts at communication would become more comprehensible. She should never be afraid.

Continuing the note, I detailed specific facts concerning my personal visit with Eliza Faith. I conveyed how her grandmother was crying when I approached the bench. Digressing momentarily, I told Faith how she bore a remarkable resemblance to her grandmother. Eliza Faith knew about Faith's tragedies. She wanted to help, but barriers impeded her efforts. She turned to me for necessary support and inspiration. She felt as though I would provide the key to reopen Faith's heart.

I wrote with particular clarity how Eliza Faith revealed herself at the large cross in Groom, Texas. Through God, she was prodding me to journey east. When I was heading in that direction, the vision once again appeared at the cross in an effort to thank me. As tears formed in my eyes, I recalled the last visit from her to my grandparents' graves. She appeared to want to hug and thank me for my extraordinary effort to save Faith. God clearly had a hand in these surreal events.

I finally mentioned how Eliza Faith described the bond she and Faith had established at birth. I recounted how Eliza Faith held her granddaughter for the first time. I included how her grandmother would attend church with Faith, recite bible verses, and sing a particular hymn to her that would make her smile. Seeing the moon and stars on a warm night was a blessing for Faith. By reiterating this information, Faith had to acknowledge I had visited her grandmother. I concluded the first part of my note by declaring that Faith had an incredible grandmother.

Before continuing to the second part of Faith's note, I decided to take a break. I would have most of the day to complete the note and deliver it to Anna. Afterwards, I would have time to wait for a response. While I was hoping I might receive a phone call, I remained pessimistic considering Faith's attitude the last time I saw her. I said a prayer that God would provide the comfort to accept any response that was forthcoming.

As I mentally outlined the remainder of the note, I quickly purchased a sub and juice at a nearby eatery. When I returned to my truck, I retrieved the list that Eliza Faith had given to me. I ate while I reviewed this writing. While the list was worn, its contents remained clearly legible. This writing consisted of numerous bible verses and references. It clearly resembled the type of list my grandmother provided to me when I was younger.

My desire was to organize some of these verses to clearly emphasize my points to Faith. She may have already heard these verses before directly through Eliza Faith's own mouth. By conveying these points succinctly with their relevance, Faith could vividly apply the effect of these divine words to her life. It was an insufficient argument merely to recite these verses. Like a dagger through an evil animal, I had to construct an intense blade to cut away Faith's pronounced misery.

Through adversity, God will provide the necessary compassion, hope, and understanding to endure. We never walk alone. My first bible verse reflected this point:

The eternal God is thy refuge, and underneath are the everlasting arms; and He shall thrust out the enemy from before thee; and shall say, Destroy them. Deuteronomy 33:27.

It was vital that Faith reestablish her firm connection with God. He would provide the vital link to overcome this crisis. She could then eradicate the sadness that was consuming her.

Along with His vast and vital presence, God wants every living being to understand He has great plans for everyone. These plans do not include just tragedies. They also include plans with blessings of hope and inspiration. The second verse I included incorporated this thought:

"For I know the plans I have for you," declares the Lord," plans to prosper you and not to harm you, plans to give you hope and a future." Jeremiah 29:11.

I wanted to emphasize that, while Faith may be enduring hardships now, God had a future plan which included significant blessings for her and her loved ones. The moment of crisis would surely pass. I reminded myself of the old saying, "There is always light at the end of the tunnel."

Through faith and hope comes inspiration and strength. God provides this strength through our belief in Him. What one person cannot accomplish alone, God's presence combines with our spirit to create an unparalleled combative force to overcome any hardship. The next verse conveyed this aspect:

But they that wait upon the Lord shall renew their strength; they shall mount up with wings as eagles; they shall run, and not be weary; and they shall walk and not faint. Isaiah 40:31.

By reaffirming her belief in God coupled with great plans God has promised, I wrote that Faith had the ability to fly above the clouds of any developing calamity. Hope would provide the cure.

The last two verses I included in Faith's note related similar issues and sentiments. The first verse reflected how one should reach for an inner strength and resilience to move beyond any tragedy that has occurred. We should not give up. God would be a formidable ally in recovering from pain associated with loss. The first of these two verses read:

We are afflicted in every way, but not crushed; perplexed, but not driven to despair; persecuted, but not forsaken; struck down, but not destroyed; 2 Corinthians 4:8-9.

Fate had beaten down Faith's morale with many difficult tragedies. It was impossible to comprehend the extent of this adversity to Faith's soul. However, as easy as it was to undergo these experiences, God would provide the bridge for happier and more prosperous times.

The final verse epitomized the essence of Faith's actual situation.

This verse stated:

When the righteous cry for help, the Lord hears and delivers them out of all their troubles. The Lord is near to the brokenhearted and saves the crushed in spirit. Many are the afflictions of the righteous, but the Lord delivers him out of them all. Psalms 34:17-19.

I recounted the losses Faith had experienced: her grandmother, her miscarriage, Baby Gabe, her husband Gabe, and finally her involvement in the near-fatal traffic accident. I told Faith that while I empathize with her intense sadness, she would be able to feel the intense joy when times improved. In short, she would really appreciate the good times by enduring through the bad. I felt all these verses conveyed a concise and significant point I needed Faith to see. I manifested a sigh of relief with the completion of this segment of Faith's note.

Before returning Eliza Faith's list to a protective plastic cover I had in my shirt pocket, I noticed something I had yet to observe with this list. Beyond the verses were the following words: "Recipe-cookies." Examining the list further, this writing appeared to include the ingredients contained in a recipe for butterscotch cookies and how to bake them. Clearly this information consisted of how to make Faith's grandmother's famous cookies. I had to find the time to personally make these precious sweets. I was certain the opportunity would provide an additional weapon to overcome Faith's depression.

After a moment of meditation, I commenced writing the third part of Faith's note. Its effect was the most uncertain part of this note. The success of my plan hinged on Faith's reaction. I was confident a positive answer would fill the abyss of Faith's depression. I prayed that God would see His will was done.

The Last Part of Faith's Note: The Request

When I was enthralled in the mist with Eliza Faith, I was captivated by this woman's charm and electricity. She had an allure that I had never seen. I genuinely felt that if Faith had actual exposure to her presence again, this connection would turn the tide to Faith's negative emotions. How could I get these two together?

I switched CDs to the Christian music composition that I listened to during my first drive to California. Since I thought about how special it would be to have a passenger on my next run, I needed to ask Faith to ride with me. Taking her away from all the sadness would inject a healthy dose of relaxation and be a necessary distraction in her life. My understanding was that she had not been away from Nashville. Since the load destination would return me to Nashville, she would not be gone very long.

I emphasized that I had noble intentions. I had been heartbroken hearing about all of Faith's recent tragedies. My purpose in requesting her presence was simple. I wanted to be a guide to direct her to a happier, more fulfilling life. I merely wanted her to smile again.

Piecing the puzzle together like I had learned from God through Miri, I formulated a driving schedule. My plan was to stop again in Groom, Texas, at the cross. I needed Faith to experience the location where I encountered the vivid image of her grandmother. I experienced her presence stronger there than any other place except dreaming of her in the mist. I conveyed this fact in the note. By not possessing fear, she might experience the presence of her grandmother again. It was worth the effort to make this suggestion.

My final plan to help Faith was complete. I constructed an intense note that included my experiences with her grandmother. She loved Eliza Faith like no other person in her life. I included bible verses defining their relevance. This inspirational prose would be easy for Faith to comprehend. Finally, I requested Faith to accompany me on my next drive. All my efforts hinged on a positive response. I would not know how to react if she said no. Yet I felt God would provide the answer, notwithstanding the nature of her response.

Upon completion of the note, I looked out the passenger window of my truck. The rain had almost completely stopped. It was at that moment that an extraordinary sight appeared. I witnessed the formation of a double rainbow. I almost lost my breath. In that instance, I experienced God's presence, and I knew He was guiding me in the right direction.

CHAPTER 18

Faith's Reaction to the
Note and the Cookies

My Attempt to Bake Eliza Faith's Cookies

Before delivering my note to Anna to give to Faith, I had two additional responsibilities. Since I had the recipe for Faith's grandmother's famous butterscotch cookies, I wanted to try to bake a batch. I could deliver this batch with the note. My idea would offer extra proof of my contact with her grandmother. Such proof might provide an additional impetus for Faith to travel west with me.

Near the truck stop, I had seen a decent motel complex at an affordable cost. Their rooms would offer a variety of amenities. From a complimentary continental breakfast with free coffee to satellite television to kitchenettes, their services were very attractive to a weary traveler anxious to unwind. It was at this location that I decided to make my cooking attempt. My first responsibility was to get a room there for the evening.

A medium-sized grocery store occupied the lot across the street. My second responsibility was to begin purchasing necessary items for my cooking quest. Since I was a trucker with little time to cook, this venture would indeed be novel for me. Even during my marriage, Jennifer cooked all the meals. My expertise rested in merely placing items in a microwave to heat up. I was excited at the prospect of trying something as new and important as baking these special cookies.

First, I purchased the utensils I would need. I required bowls and a spatula to mix the ingredients. I would also need a baking sheet to place the cookies. Finally, I would need the variety of ingredients Eliza Faith wrote on her list.

These ingredients included: butter, brown sugar, granulated sugar, light corn syrup, eggs, vanilla extract, flour, nonfat milk powder, kosher salt, baking powder, baking soda, and butterscotch chips. However, there was a spice of which I lacked familiarity included at the end. I asked a nearby grocery clerk what this was. She explained that this was a type of rare spice that bakers typically included in recipes to provide a different, more flavorful taste. After this explanation, I firmly believed I had discovered the main secret ingredient which made Eliza Faith's cookies so delectable.

After returning to my room, I organized my supplies on a counter. I began following Eliza Faith's instructions on the list. After this preparation and placing the cookies on the sheet, I placed the sheet in the oven. I would need to let them bake for approximately 15 minutes. After a few minutes, I detected an appealing aroma coming from the oven. I knew without any doubt how good and special these cookies would be after baking.

During the time these cookies were in the oven, I made a brief phone call to Charles and Sarah. I had not heard much from them lately. I wanted to inquire how they were doing. I was surprised when someone answered after a solitary ring. It was Charles.

He commented that he and Sarah had been under intense stress with Faith.

They had the ominous thought that Faith would try to end her life. The mental pressure had gotten that great. He was glad that I called. He reiterated what he had once told me: I was sent by God to help Faith endure through this difficult time. All I said was that I just desired in the worst way to assist Faith through this troubled time.

After a moment of silence, I told Charles I had something important to tell him. I needed his approval for what I was proceeding to attempt. I conveyed information about my new load assignment. However, I emphasized the note I had written and its contents. I inquired if he would approve of my attempt to take Faith on a trip. I briefly mentioned the cross, Eliza Faith, and my encounters with Faith's grandmother. I indicated that Faith had nothing to lose by my request. In fact, this attempt might be what God required to alleviate her wounded heart.

Charles did not hesitate. He stated he clearly trusted me. He believed I had slowly been working unseen wonders on Faith's heart. He also sincerely believed I had communicated with Eliza Faith. One little breakthrough would provide a flood like a hole in a dam for the depression ensnaring Faith's heart. He concluded the call by saying to be safe, keep in touch, and let him know of any progress I was making with Faith. As he hung up, I began to realize what an impact I was having on each member of this precious, simple family.

The timer on my stove began ringing. The cookies were done. I took them out of the oven and placed the baking sheet on the stove to cool.

Subsequently, I began making a second batch to take with us on our excursion. When the cookies completely cooled, I took one as a sample. I had no idea what I had just finished. Biting into this cookie, I could see why Gabe would comment that these were the finest cookies he had ever tasted.

The Delivery of the Note

After finishing my baking masterpiece, I lay down briefly for a little nap. When I awoke, I felt reinvigorated. I opened the door for some fresh air. A cool wind hit my face as the sun was setting in the distance. I knew I was beginning to run out of time. I would need to deliver the note to Faith soon.

I placed the letter in an envelope. I sealed the envelope and placed Faith's name in bold capital letters on the outside. Below her name, I included a bible verse appropriate for the way I seemed to feel:

Let all that you do be done in love. 1 Corinthians 16:14.

I was hoping that I was not too forward in my thoughts. Nonetheless, I had to show Faith how attached to her I was getting during the short time I knew her. I continued having the thought that I could not bear to see her die.

I packed the cookies neatly in a plastic container. I placed a sticky note on the outside proclaiming that Faith's grandmother had assisted me in producing the yummy treats. I continued to be hopeful that this endeavor would compel Faith to take the pertinent trip together with me. If so, I remained confident that God would reveal his intention during these critical moments.

I finally put the cookies in a paper sack, softly placing the envelope with Faith's note on the top. I was very careful to make sure the cookies were intact and incapable of shifting. I felt that I was nearing the end of my mission. The consequence would rest in God's hands.

I grabbed the sack and walked slowly to my truck. Outside, I heard birds happily chirping in the wind. It reminded me of my ventures in the mist where I met Miri, Faith, and, most importantly, her grandmother. A smile slowly overtook my face. I was subsumed by a feeling of gratification and inspiration I had never experienced. I opened the driver door, carefully placed the note and cookies next to the driver's seat, started the truck, and eagerly began driving to the hospital.

In a matter of minutes, I arrived at the hospital. Reversing the steps I took to place the note and cookies in my truck, I removed them with similar care. I exited the truck, locked the door, and proceeded to walk to the hospital entrance. I felt a similar feeling to when I first arrived to meet Faith. My throat became dry, my heart seemed to palpitate, and my hands developed a sweat that seemed to result from my anxiety. I really did not know what to expect. I said a brief prayer that God would help me relax during this uncertain and anxious time.

I quickly entered the hospital and approached the information center. Anna was at the desk. She smiled and greeted me as I got closer. I mentioned that she looked tired. Her response noted that, because of a shortage of reliable help, she was compelled to work a series of double shifts. Were it not for the schedule, Anna related that she would not have been present at that time. I thanked God for allowing her presence and for being able to deliver the note and cookies.

I placed the paper sack on the counter by Anna's opening in the glass enclosure. Initially, I retrieved the envelope with Faith's note. Moreover, I carefully pulled out the container with Faith's cookies. In an effort to get Anna's reaction, I insisted that she sample one. She loved sweets and did not hesitate to take one.

I smiled when she took a tiny bite of her cookie. The reaction on her face spoke volumes as to what she thought. I could have anticipated her response. She declared that the cookie was remarkable and the best she had ever tasted. God truly blessed me with the idea of baking these cookies. Anna inquired how I knew how to make such an exquisite treat. I responded with the comment that Faith's grandmother played a crucial role in the production of these cookies.

Anna knew that Faith's grandmother had died. How could she have played a part in helping me? Anna had a quizzical look in her eyes. To clarify this information, I retrieved the list from my shirt pocket. While I did not specify the way I possessed this list, Anna's bewilderment slowly dissipated. After her last bite, she smiled at me again. Anna believed there was no possibility of Faith turning away from me after tasting these cookies.

Anna returned the cookies and the note to the paper bag. She stated she would deliver these items in approximately one hour when she made some rounds. She kindly told me she would contact me when they were delivered. Finally, she would let me know Faith's reaction and if a response was forthcoming. I expressed my appreciation and smiled as I reversed my direction to depart from the hospital.

After delivering the note, I experienced a sense of relief at my effort. It felt as though thousands of bricks were simultaneously removed from my shoulders. While I seemed pleased with what I had done, all I could do now was wait. I had no idea what Faith's reaction would entail. Would her emotions change? Would her depression and suicidal thoughts continue? Only God and time would pave the path to the answers to these and other questions.

Faith's Absent Reaction

I returned to my truck. Upon opening the door, I sat quietly in the driver's seat for a brief moment. I closed my eyes as I silently prayed and meditated. Tears slowly formed in my tired eyes. While I wanted Faith to completely recover, I had a selfish thought materialize in my mind. I had a yearning for the true romantic worldly love that had eluded my grasp during my life. Maybe I was attaching myself too tightly to Faith when I did not really understand her.

I continued this thought after I returned to my room. I experienced a lot during my marriage to Jennifer. However, our sudden relationship was not the true love I hungered for. Her anxiety alone created the barrier to a lasting relationship. I had yet to possess the knowledge to fix the problem. I would truly be alone when our divorce became final. I prayed that God would comfort me with my empty heart.

These thoughts carried on after I decided to lie down in bed. I turned on the television to create a distraction from getting too immersed in my thoughts. No matter what I did, I could not manage to relax. Faith and the possibility of true love weighed heavily on my mind.

Eventually, my phone started ringing. Anna was calling. I immediately responded. Anna had given the paper bag directly to Faith. Her parents were in the room at the time. Faith had little opportunity to respond. At that moment, she was provided with a mild tranquilizer to make her sleep. Anna asked me to be patient for a response. An immediate response was not possible. I told Anna I understood. Finally, Anna wanted me to rest and stated she would call me tomorrow. After these words, we hung up.

I continued to lie back, staring at the ceiling. I recognized that this night would pass by slowly. Occasionally, I would have fleeting recollections of past girls I had dated. In my mental review, I was able to discern that the minimal time I was with these girls was seriously lacking in substantial quality time for the formation of true love. A significant amount of time is warranted merely to get acquainted with a dating partner. One can learn a great deal through time, both good and bad. If I truly embarked on a relationship with Faith, I wanted to commit to doing it the right way. It would take time for a relationship to develop and blossom.

I managed to doze off a little after this thought. Later, when my mouth became dry, I got up to pour myself a glass of water. Realizing I had not eaten, I removed a plastic bag from the refrigerator with a sandwich I had prepared when I was baking Faith's cookies. I looked at the digital clock on the small table beside the bed. The time was 3:00 a.m.

After consuming this snack with some more water, I sat in a lounge chair next to the bed. I thought about how my first intense relationship occurred when I was attending law school. She was pretty, petite, and very smart. It did not take long before we became physically intimate.

However, our relationship only lasted for a few months. The day after my birthday, she informed me she was breaking up. An old flame had returned to her life from military service. I still wanted us to be friends. She hesitated. After that moment, I never saw her again. I never visualized Faith as a sex object. I thought it prudent to save this thought until we were married, if our relationship progressed to that step. With my faith, that time would be the right time to indulge in order to really convey our love for each other.

I relived my encounter with Crystal at the Ontario truck stop. I recalled the image appearing to resemble Miri. She appeared to mouth one word in my direction: "NO!" I was sure God was directing me to abstain from physical intimacy until after marriage. Otherwise, the meaning of sex would be lost. I would be partaking in the motion purely for gratification. I would lose the meaning of true love by prematurely indulging in a sacred act. I was overwhelmed by how I was organizing my thoughts. God was instrumental in forcing my eyes to see light at the end of a tunnel.

Finally, I was able to enter a deep, relaxing slumber. When my eyes opened, the brightness of the day filled the room. I did not have to worry about leaving immediately. As I explained to the motel clerk that I was a trucker, I was able to reserve the room until I left in the evening. Now the time on my clock showed 1:00 p.m.

Sensing I was running out of time, I called Anna. I told her I would be leaving within the next several hours. I explained that I wanted Faith to ride with me. It was a short haul that would only take a few days to run. I told Anna to tell Faith that I would be waiting for her near the emergency room entrance. I would be driving the truck with a shiny Sunshine Logistics logo. If I did not see her at 9:00 p.m., I would assume she did not want to go. However, I emphatically stated to Anna that I would try calling Faith when I returned to Nashville. Anna said she would provide this information to Faith immediately after the doctor finished her evaluation. I sensed my voice start to crack as I concluded the call. Time was my worthy adversary.

I started preparing for my departure. I finished a load of laundry. I neatly folded these items while organizing my clothes in a small hamper behind the driver's seat of the truck. I reorganized the contents of my cooler after purchasing new supplies at the local grocery store. I also organized my CDs adeptly in a travel case. Finally, I prepared a nice bunk for Faith to sleep if she decided to go. After cleaning inside my truck, I decided to return to the room to relax.

I sat up in bed and turned on the television. I left the channel on a wildlife station. I was uninterested in the discussion since I was preoccupied with my impending trip. I ordered a pizza for delivery to the room. At that point, I had not heard anything from Anna.

Time appeared to be speeding along faster than I perceived. The hours passed, and my phone was silent. After eating the pizza and taking another nap, the moment of truth began to rapidly approach. The time the clock illuminated was now 7:30 p.m.

I realized I had little time before leaving Nashville. With or without Faith, I was driving toward Albuquerque. I took a quick shower to wake up completely. Later, I walked into the motel lobby to pour myself a fresh cup of coffee. All that time, I wondered how Faith was. How did her evaluation fare? Was there an answer to eradicate Faith's depression? My mind and heart were completely turned over to the will of God.

As 9:00 p.m. approached, I made sure I was not leaving anything in the room. I took my key to the front desk, indicating I was leaving. The motel clerk hoped I enjoyed my stay and wished me well on my excursion. Soon, I climbed into the truck, started the engine, and meditated for a few minutes.

The time had come for me to get a decision from Faith. While I was optimistic she would be waiting for me, I was expecting the worst. The thought of traveling alone with me might be too much for her heart to digest. I placed the truck in gear as I slowly exited the motel parking lot en route to the hospital.

As I pulled into the hospital lot across from the emergency room, I only observed a man in a wheelchair being assisted into a car. No other activity was evident. The time was a few minutes before 9 p.m. I had a little time, so I decided to shut off my engine and wait. My true desire was to see Faith being wheeled in the direction of my truck. My longing to help her was as strong as it had ever been. I was willing to wait a little longer in the event she was not discharged immediately.

During my wait, I thought about my first visit to see Faith. She appeared excited to see me for the first time. Additionally, on at least a few occasions, she stated she thought I reminded her of Gabe. I thought about her room number: room 316. This thought made me recall a bible verse:

> *For God so loved the world, that He gave His only begotten Son, that whosoever believeth in Him shall not perish, but have everlasting life.*
> *John 3:16.*

I knew God had been directing my life down His divine path. Regardless of whether I saw Faith, His hands would continue pushing me to the revelations He wished me to discover. I knew I would experience pain by not seeing Faith; however, God would temper this pain through the directions He was giving me.

Approximately twenty minutes had passed. Still, there was no sign of Faith. I could not afford to wait any longer if I wanted to deliver my new load. I said a quick prayer for God's strength. I started my truck. I looked around and gradually figured it was inevitable that I would leave without Faith. I was heartbroken when I placed the truck in gear to begin the lengthy drive to New Mexico. I slowly accelerated the truck toward the hospital exit. I realized I was experiencing my worst fear.

CHAPTER 19

Journey Towards a New Reality with Faith

Faith Comes After All

I continued my slow drive to the hospital exit. I had to maneuver by the emergency entrance before reaching this exit. Tears began slowly running down my cheeks. I was truly heartbroken by leaving Faith behind. As I began to pray, I became distracted by a sound emanating from the rear of my semi.

I looked toward the passenger mirror, hoping to visualize what was causing this sound. I thought the source of this sound was a woman yelling behind me. Squinting my eyes, I noticed in the mirror a woman walking hastily toward my truck. I slowed my vehicle and was finally able to discern who this person was.

Faith was waving for me to stop.

I was in complete shock. After stopping my rig, I noticed Charles and Sarah at the emergency entrance. They were standing by a few bags.

As Faith approached, I observed tears in her eyes. These tears made me cry. Faith said she wanted to come with me. As we embraced, I told her I was praying I would not have to leave without her.

After a few minutes, Charles and Sarah arrived with Faith's luggage. They greeted me with a smile. Charles shook my hand. He mentioned his sincere gratitude for the impact I was having on his family. He added that he wanted me to take care of Faith. I told him I would keep them regularly informed concerning Faith's condition. Shortly thereafter, they said polite farewells to Faith and me as they began walking in the reverse direction.

I helped Faith climb into the truck. She stated that she was sleepy because of another recently administered tranquilizer. I quickly showed her the bunk I had made for her. Since my truck almost felt like it was riding on air when moving, I told her she should have little difficulty resting. With her head nestled against a pillow, I softly tucked her in under a little blanket I had placed on the bunk. Finally, I added that if she needed anything, she could let me know. I understood then that God was blessing me with her presence. It would be my responsibility to take care of her. I had no plans to let either God or Faith down as I continued this amazing journey.

I started the engine and slowly began pulling away from the hospital. It would be a long trip to Albuquerque. It would take a few days for me to reach this destination. During this time, God would provide the opportunity for me to get to know Faith. Furthermore, I would be stopping at the cross. Hopefully, my plan for Faith to visit with her grandmother would be the ultimate dagger to alleviate Faith's depression. The fact that Faith was with me during this trip was a significant step to the accomplishment of my plan.

Faith and Memphis

After exiting the hospital, I began driving toward the freeway. In the distance, I observed a vivid full moon above the horizon. I sensed this was another sign that God was watching over Faith and me as we pulled onto the freeway. Since Faith seemed very tired, I would be alone with my thoughts for the first part of this drive. Nonetheless, I realized there would be plenty of time for me to converse with Faith.

As it was getting late, traffic would be slow until I got close to Memphis. I planned to take a brief rest stop by the Mississippi River when I arrived. At that time, I contemplated waking Faith briefly to see if she needed anything. In the back of my mind, I wanted to see her reaction to the river and the lights of Memphis. I suppose I wanted to make a good impression so she would continue being distracted from her problems.

Memphis remained over three hours away. I reached into my cooler to get a juice. I also turned the radio to a classical station. I kept the volume low, so I did not disturb Faith. I was trying to make this trip feel more like a vacation for both of us than work. Still, I remained cognizant of the enormous responsibility of getting my load and returning to Nashville.

During the drive to Memphis, I began to relive specific aspects of this incredible adventure. The visit with Miri in the mist, along with observing the images of Eliza Faith, captivated my attention. However, another obscure thought entered my mind. This thought dealt with Faith and my effort to discover true love.

Miri mentioned I had to trust my faith when we first met. Yet I needed to be patient. God would provide a path with significant changes in the future. It was clear I longed for the true love of my life. Since I had shown a sensitivity to gradually fit together the pieces to God's great puzzle, was Faith the missing link to connect all these pieces?

With my growing empathy for her needs, I truly felt I was the person to provide love and support not only during this gloomy time, but also for the rest of her life. I had no plans to abandon our friendship.

The trek to Memphis was unremarkable. However, a fleeting thought concerning my Ontario trip entered my consciousness. I remembered the billboard I had seen. I recalled intensely what this particular sign said: Faith will provide your answers. It became imperative that, since Faith was with me, I had to pay attention to every verbal and nonverbal suggestion she provided. God would provide the answers through my simple observations. I could hardly wait for Faith to wake to begin this process.

Traffic started to increase significantly as I approached the outskirts of Memphis. I was looking forward to resting as well as briefly talking to Faith. I turned the volume down on the radio and rolled down my window. I desired to feel the cool air of the night hitting my face. It was at that moment that I had another incredible experience.

I heard a sound permeate throughout the cab of my truck. It sounded like a woman's voice. I briefly glanced at Faith. The words were coming from her mouth. She appeared to be mumbling in her sleep.

She appeared to be calling me. I was taken aback by this strange turn of events. The words sounded eerily similar to the sound of the voice I heard driving through the desert, leaving Phoenix for Ontario. God was putting the colors on the canvas for the ultimate painting He wished me to witness.

When my shock diminished, I was slowly pulling into the rest stop by the mighty Mississippi. I stopped the rig and sighed. I turned toward the bunk and tapped Faith lightly on the shoulder. I wanted to make sure I was doing everything I could to keep her comfortable. I was gradually starting to sense she had to be the true love God intended me to find.

She slowly started to wake as my gentle tapping continued. As her eyes opened, she was very inquisitive. Where were we? When would we be at the cross that I had spoken so reverently of? I only said that we were taking a break. We were in Memphis, and I wanted to see if she wanted to go for a short walk with me. Maybe the fresh southern Memphis air would provide a spark to her cheerful personality.

Without hesitation, she accepted my offer. While she did not seem very cheerful, she did not seem as depressed as I had seen her. She mentioned that her evaluation manifested positive tones. Her attending physician was convinced that, through a mild antidepressant, mild tranquilizers to be used as necessary, along with intensive counseling, the prospect was good that Faith would return to her more sparkling self with the passage of a little time. My heart became warm after hearing this news.

Continuing with her oratory, she stated that she thought I would leave without her. Although she was discharged, she hesitated to go with me since she continued to be depressed about everything she was enduring.

However, one event changed her mind. She reviewed the note I had provided. While that glance did not in and of itself affect her decision, she saw the container. She discovered the cookies as she slowly opened the plastic lid. Since she was a little hungry for a snack, considering her evaluation and the hospital food she had been subjected to, she bit into this cookie. She was left speechless. The taste reminded her so much of the cookies her grandmother used to bake. Her only inquiry was where these cookies came from.

I mouthed a quiet prayer of thanks to God as Faith said these words.

I simply told her that I had gotten her grandmother's recipe and was able to manufacture a close facsimile of these cookies. I told her that those butterscotch cookies were the best I had ever tasted. I could almost sense a smile starting to grow on Faith's face. While it was fleeting, this sense was gone like cars passing by me on the freeway. However, I was really beginning to believe my efforts were very slowly and steadily working positive dividends.

We continued walking by the river, feeling the nighttime air. We could see the reflection of the lights from the city illuminating the ripples from the watery vastness. Farther down, we observed a family of ducks at the river's edge, where there was a calmness. This family had a mother and father duck as well as two babies. Once again, I could almost sense a smile trying to cover Faith's face.

While Faith seemed to enjoy the walk, she stated that she was beginning to tire again. We reversed direction and returned to the truck. She climbed back into her bunk. At the same time, I returned to the driver's seat. I provided another cookie for her with a juice for her to drink.

I sensed something in the air that would provide a breakthrough for what I was attempting to accomplish with Faith. After consuming our treats, I told her we had over nine hours before we would be at the cross. I also told Faith that I was hopeful of what she would experience once we arrived. Another smile seemed to swim to the surface of her tired face; however, it did not seem to quite make it. I reached over, tucked her gently under the blanket, smiled, and finally kissed her on the cheek. After I returned to the driver's seat with my own blanket, we both closed our eyes for a well-deserved slumber.

Onward to the Cross

When I finally awoke, I observed it was light outside. What seemed to be a short respite turned out to be a few hours. I looked at Faith, and she continued to rest peacefully. The break would be sufficient for the resumption of the trip. I had plans to be near the cross that evening. The following morning, I wanted Faith to see this landmark. After starting the engine, I began accelerating to return to the interstate.

Soon, I found myself traveling through Arkansas. At that time, Faith had become conscious from her slumber. She wanted to ride in the front seat. Without hesitation, I told her to come to the passenger seat and put on the seatbelt. While I could not detect a sense of depression, I did not observe an affirmation that her spirits were uplifted. I thought that the experience now would provide the perfect opportunity to truly get to know more about Faith and her innermost feelings.

My first topic concerned Faith's calling my name in her sleep. I asked her if she knew what I was referring to. Faith had a simple response. She was dreaming, and she remained in her hospital bed. She was unable to see me and figured I had left without her. She was calling for me in an effort to try to get me to come to her. Yet I never did. At that point, she felt me tapping her shoulder.

I thanked God again. This event made me feel that Faith had some sort of growing bond with me. My heart warmed at this thought. I felt I was proceeding to develop a closer attachment to this special woman. I prayed that God would let this feeling continue.

The distance from Memphis to Little Rock is relatively short. We continued small talk until we arrived in Little Rock. I had mentioned Jennifer, our problems, and our ultimate pursuit of the divorce. Faith seemed to display a genuine interest in this topic. When asked why I had not left her, knowing the magnitude of her tragedies, I had a clear and succinct response. I stated that I had failed my marriage and left when it was more important to fight for someone you had developed feelings for. I emphasized that I would never leave Faith. I sincerely thought I detected a tear forming in one of her now revived eyes.

Upon entering Little Rock, we decided to stop to get something to eat. First, I stopped at a truck stop where Faith was able to shower, change clothes, and revive herself. Next, we continued to a local restaurant which I had visited many times as a boy when my grandparents took me to Tennessee. While the time was not really breakfast nor considered lunchtime, I decided to order a southwest-style omelet. Following my lead, Faith decided to order the same. Other than in her relationship with Gabe, no one had ever treated her the way I had from the outset of our relationship.

While our focus was on our meal, Faith did have something enlightening to say about when we were walking by the river. This walk reminded her of the times she and Baby Gabe would take similar walks in Nashville. Further, seeing the ducks reminded her of the family and simple life she regularly craved. Fortunately, at no time did Faith seem to be sinking into the intense depression I had seen. I sensed Faith was making progress in her bout with her feelings of sadness.

Faith inquired as to the reason I did not have a family. I answered her with the comment that God had not blessed me with any children in my marriage. I did have the two stepchildren; although it was not the same as having my own, I loved them as if they were my own flesh and blood. Because of my schedule at work, I was not able to spend quality time with Jennifer and her children like I wanted.

After finishing our meal, we returned to the freeway. Our conversation continued. It had not yet been a part of God's plan for me to have my own children. Nevertheless, I loved children and would welcome a baby in the future if it were God's will. Maybe not having children with Jennifer was a blessing. There would be no children exposed to the friction, tension, and division divorce often causes.

At that point, Faith grew silent. She began looking out the window at the view as we drove through a rural area. She appeared deep in thought when I asked her what she was thinking about. She turned toward me, and we made brief eye contact. There was a sense of contentment radiating from her face.

Faith responded with an answer I thought might be forthcoming. She wanted a simple life with a simple family. She yearned to marry again despite her depression. Yet she never thought she would ever meet a man like Gabe. Her voice started to crack as she added that I was attractive to her because I possessed Gabe's temperament and personality. My personality, however, tended to go a bit further with my unrelenting compassion and inspiration.

Our conversation continued as we neared Fort Smith. I told Faith that I would see her through this dark hour regardless of the circumstances. Thereafter, I wanted to remain an integral part of her life. I wanted to share her experiences with even happier moments.

Sensing we might be on the same wavelength emotionally, I smiled at her. At that moment, I really thought I had finally observed a faint smile overtake her face. I reached over to briefly squeeze her hand.

Time passed, and we were traveling through Oklahoma. Before arriving near Oklahoma City, I asked Faith if she would like to listen to a Christian CD. She responded positively and selected the same CD I had listened to on my first run to Ontario. She seemed to be very relaxed and content at this point.

As I was deep in reflection, I heard Faith cry out. I looked over at her with a concerned frown. Faith asked me to look. She asked me if I could see them. Since I was driving, I could only glance but pay little attention to what had caught her vision. She apologized and said she had seen a mother and father rabbit with two bunnies. I was amused by these words. I smiled. I told her there were meanings to everything in life. It was all part of God's plan. Even these rabbits had a meaning that God would eventually attach significance to us. Immediately, a big grin appeared on Faith's face.

Faith started talking again. She said she was missing her mother, the flower shop, and Sarabeth. Sarabeth was her aunt. She was the younger sister of her mother. That revelation would indicate why Sarabeth looked so similar to Sarah. This was another piece of the puzzle God desired to reveal to me. As we approached Oklahoma City, Faith asked me if I had observed the billboard advertising the flower shop. I nodded. She clarified that the woman holding the flowers was supposed to represent her mother. The twin girls were depictions of her and her sister, Miranda. The final brush of paint on the canvas was almost applied. The last step would be to find the lasting happiness Faith craved.

The remainder of the journey to the cross was quiet, relaxing, and uneventful. We briefly stopped to rest at an Oklahoma City truck stop. I made a couple of sandwiches with chips on paper plates and included one of the cookies I brought. Faith displayed no obvious signs of the depression that had devastated her mind. I also called Charles and Sarah to let them know the status. They only said that they had no doubts about my ability to help their daughter. After Faith talked for a few minutes, we finished our meal and prepared for the remainder of God's adventure.

After a few more hours, we arrived at a motel near Groom and the cross. Both of us were weary from the all-day drive. By that time, I had gotten to know Faith better than ever. I reserved a room with separate single beds. I told Faith that we would visit the cross at morning's first light. At that moment, she would see her grandmother.

Faith was excited at the prospect. After tucking her in, kissing her on the cheek, and saying a prayer, I told her to rest peacefully. The next morning would be another moment of truth. When I turned out the lights, Faith quietly declared that she was proud I was with her and a part of her life. I had a sense of satisfaction at my efforts. I curled into my bed after setting a digital clock, placed a blanket over me, and soon drifted away into a deep sleep.

CHAPTER 20

Faith and her Grandmother at the Cross

The Initial Failure at the Cross

I heard Faith moving in the room before the alarm sounded. Her hair appeared wet, and she was dressed in fresh clothes. Apparently, she must have taken a shower. The soft fragrance of perfume permeated my senses. I lifted my head to discern what she was doing. My thought was that she was anxious to visit the cross.

Sitting on the edge of her bed, she glanced over at me. Our eyes met once again. She apologized for waking me. She started staring at the locket around her neck. After a brief silence, she wanted to know if she would see her beloved grandmother soon. My only response was that God would provide the answer. Faith needed to prepare herself mentally if Eliza Faith did not make an appearance.

Faith walked over to my bed as I placed my feet on the floor. With the full redness of her lips, she kissed my forehead. She again mentioned how grateful she was that we were together. She firmly believed that she would see her grandmother. She emphatically declared that I had come too far to let her down. God and my inspiration were fueling her heart to overcome life's adverse challenges.

I smiled at her. I stood up and embraced her tightly. No matter what transpired, this snapshot would forever be captured in my mind. My feelings were growing deeper for this simple southern gal. I whispered in her ear that God would show us both the path we needed to walk. Hopefully, the journey would be together. An appearance by her grandmother would provide a monster step in the right direction.

I told her I needed to get ready for the important drive to the cross. I too showered quickly, got dressed, and asked her if she wanted breakfast. She interjected that she was not hungry. However, she took a little fruit that I had placed in my cooler. I likewise cut an apple into thin slices that I had provided for the trip. We both had a nervous sensitivity as to what was about to happen. After consuming our fruit, we embraced again. I said a prayer that God would direct us to where He desired. I added for Him to provide comfort and understanding at the cross. Finally, I concluded by asking God to keep us safe and cradled in His arms for the rest of the day. I wanted God to help Faith demolish her depression once and for all.

Faith and I returned to my truck. After buckling in, we resumed the short 20-minute drive to the cross. I heard Faith sigh deeply as we saw the cross from a distance. She had never imagined this cross was that large. It took a moment for Faith to catch her breath. I noticed she was holding and clutching her locket tightly.

We pulled into an empty lot. Turning to the east, we observed the sun poking above the horizon. I believe neither of us had preconceived expectations as to what was about to occur. Would Eliza Faith make another appearance in this locale?

Nothing happened after a twenty-minute wait. Regrettably, I informed Faith that in less than an hour, I would have to start the five- hour drive to Albuquerque. She nodded. Tears started to form in her eyes as she continued her firm grasp on the locket.

After I mumbled a low prayer, an image eventually started to appear. Unfortunately, the image was very faint. Faith and I exited the truck to investigate the apparition. The image definitely resembled Faith's grandmother. Faith let out a loud cry calling for her grandmother. I sincerely believed she was mesmerized by the moment of this unforgettable experience. Both Faith and her grandmother simultaneously reached out their arms in an effort to grasp hands. However, just as quickly as the image appeared, it was gone. Faith could only stand there in shock.

Eliza Faith was gone. I tried to comfort Faith by putting my arm around her shoulder. She clutched my right hand with her left. I recited a few of the bible verses I had previously provided. We still had a little time to see if the image would reappear. I tried to convince Faith to eliminate all doubt concerning her observation. God would take care of both of us.

We silently stood by the cross and waited. Ten minutes passed. Nothing happened. Another fifteen minutes and still no activity emerged. With tears in my eyes, I quietly told Faith we had to leave. I started to be pressed for time to make a timely run to Albuquerque.

Taking her hands and turning her toward the rig, Faith trembled and started sobbing intensely. My words did not have any impact through her tears. A crisis was about to materialize. Faith fainted and fell to the ground. I prayed for God's formidable strength during this crucial moment.

I lifted Faith in my arms and carried her to my truck. Tears were incessantly falling from my eyes. This moment was the worst I could have imagined. I was convinced Faith's depression would return with a vengeance. After administering a tranquilizer, I placed Faith in her bunk. I covered her with the blanket and told her everything would be fine. I would develop another plan. I returned to the driver's seat, took a deep breath, and started the engine.

Thereafter, I slowly accelerated toward the freeway en route to Albuquerque. We would leave the expected visions of her grandmother behind in the mirrors of time.

The Sad Return of Faith's Depression

God would never place more on my shoulders than I could bear. However, my heart ached severely at what I observed. Faith's collapse at the cross placed a heavy burden on my soul. I had to discover one last desperate measure to assist her. I had never felt as dedicated to resolving a significant problem.

Driving to pick up my load, I tried to uncover other means to encourage Faith. I softly turned on the CD Faith had been listening to. Intermittently, I would look back to see her. She seemed to be resting peacefully. However, she possessed the most somber look on her face that I had ever seen. Tears formed in my eyes at this sight.

After reaching the halfway point between the cross and Albuquerque, I decided to take a break at another truck stop. I gently tapped Faith on the shoulder. I inquired if she needed anything. She said no as she turned over and fell asleep. I entered the truck stop. Thinking about Faith, I purchased both of us a sub along with chips. I knew that Faith would eventually be hungry.

I placed this meal by her bunk. I whispered in her ear that it was there. On the paper plate, I placed one of the wrapped butterscotch cookies next to her sub. I was not going to stop my determination to make Faith happy.

I continued whispering in Faith's ear. I recited the last bible verse her grandmother included on her list:

1 Now faith is being sure of what we hope for and certain of what we do not see. 2 This is what the ancients were commended for. 3 By faith we understand that the universe was formed at God's command, so that what is seen was not made out of what was visible. Hebrews 11:1-3.

Faith seemed to try to open her eyes. This reaction was the first overt response I had seen since Faith's collapse.

I returned to the driver's seat. The journey to Albuquerque continued. Unconsciously, I began humming the hymn Eliza Faith said she had taught Faith. Instinctively, I turned to Faith. She appeared to be mouthing the words to my tones. When I stopped, Faith stopped too. I felt God was instilling in my mind the ultimate ability to resolve Faith's mental barriers.

I reached the load destination in record time. With Faith continuing to rest, I had the workers at the facility load several pallets of musical instrument parts into my trailer. Before heading to Nashville, I finally thought of one final plan to help Faith. I went to the bunk to tell her this news.

While her eyes were closed, she appeared to respond to my voice. She began clutching the locket around her neck. I conveyed how we would be returning to Groom. We would visit the cross again. Through consistent prayers, this second effort would provide the blessing we needed. Miri had said to have patience. Her grandmother would eventually appear in powerful form. Although her face showed no emotion, she reached her arms out and hugged my neck. I thanked God for this little progress.

I resumed driving east. The hours were slowly winding down to minutes. Halfway to the cross, I glanced at Faith. She had begun eating the little lunch I had provided. My heart glowed at this sight. After she finished, she rolled over and returned to her slumber. My confidence peaked. God would provide more blessings and refuse to let me down.

In the moonlight of the evening, I was pulling the truck into the parking area near the cross. The brilliant moonlight reflecting on the cross was spectacular. No one else occupied this lot. God, Faith, and I were the only ones present. I planned to rest there for the night. I did not observe any signs indicating my parking was illegal or inappropriate. I said a prayer and fell into a deep sleep, anticipating that shortly I would experience the blessing that my faith had yearned for.

The Triumphant End to Faith's Depression

After sleeping for a few hours, I looked out my window. The night continued to radiate a darkness I had never seen. Glancing at the cross, I noticed a faint light glowing in the distance. I needed to tell Faith.

Pushing her shoulder, Faith started to stir. I told her she needed to see the glow I spotted. Her response was surprising. She did not want to look. Her heart could not withstand another disappointment.

Even though I understood, I persisted in my efforts to stimulate Faith's attention. I changed the music to the newest CD I had purchased. Although the music was relaxing and inspirational, Faith demonstrated little response. She continued sleeping with a somber look on her face.

I observed the glow get brighter. I insisted that Faith pay attention to this ever-changing image. I was slowly starting to distinguish a figure in the light. Faith again showed no interest. I developed anxiety as to what to do.

Incredibly, an unexpected event blinded any other thought. The sound of Eliza Faith's hymn played on the CD. I gasped with utter surprise at this tone. Faith's eyes snapped open as if she had been administered a wake-up drug. She slowly started to sit upright. Where did this precious song come from? She began singing the words to this sacred hymn.

I removed Eliza Faith's list from my pocket. I thought I had observed the name of this song on this list. The list must have caught Faith's eyes. With a quiver in her voice, she questioned me about how I possessed this document. She appeared to be in shock at this sight.

I told her the list was presented to me by Eliza Faith herself. Faith convincingly argued that it could not be possible. Faith related that she had placed this list in her grandmother's coffin before she was buried for inspiration. Yet I was holding this list in my hands. At that moment, Faith was convinced I had actually spent time with her beloved grandmother's spirit.

We both started staring at the cross. The image became clear and crisp in the extreme darkness. Eliza Faith was beckoning for Faith to come to her. I could hear her words, desiring Faith to approach.

Faith slowly provided a response. She jumped from the rig and rapidly moved nearer to the apparition. I saw a clear smile overtake her face. Both Faith and her grandmother finally clutched hands. With tears in their eyes, Eliza Faith told her precious granddaughter to listen to her.

Eliza Faith told Faith she loved her with all her heart. She missed being with this special little girl she helped to raise. She desired to assist Faith in overcoming her adversity and depression. However, she emphasized that a kind man was present to take her place. He is the man who drove her to the cross. She had met this impressive man. Faith needed to listen to him because he was as compassionate and inspirational a man as she had ever met.

Eliza Faith resumed her words with tears. Faith was sobbing now. Eliza Faith grabbed the locket around her neck. She showed the image of Faith as a little girl. She would never forget her granddaughter. Finally, she would always be around whenever Faith would need her. At the ultimate climax of this adventure, Faith and her grandmother experienced a long, caring embrace.

Finally, this embrace was interrupted by another surreal event. Behind the cross, three images appeared simultaneously. These three images were smiling and waving at Faith. One of the images was holding a baby with its eyes open. Faith would later provide the explanation. These figures had to be those beloved family members she had lost: Gabe holding the little baby Faith miscarried, Baby Gabe, and finally her twin sister, Miri. Faith had experienced a visit from her entire lost family.

Soon, Faith and her grandmother released hands. As Eliza Faith turned to walk away, Faith stated she now understood. She would never walk alone in this world. Someone would always be around to lift her when times were good. Someone would always be around to comfort her when times were rough. She relayed how much she loved her grandmother. She affirmed that she would listen to her grandmother and take heed from the signs God would provide.

Climactically, all the images merged into one intense light that faded in the distance.

Faith approached me with a smile and a glow that I had never seen. She thanked me for saving her life. She thanked me for the visits to the cross. Finally, she thanked me for the compassion and inspiration I had provided during this tumultuous time. I was truly an angel. As we embraced, she looked into my eyes and told me she loved me.

Returning to the truck, she had one last comment: "I am so proud of you because you found me." I started the truck and headed for the return trip to Nashville.

CHAPTER 21

A Happy, Simple Life with Faith

Faith's Direction to my New Career

We would arrive in Nashville in the early afternoon of the following day. Our return trip was no longer fraught with the emotion that existed at the start. Faith's whole attitude had experienced a profound change. She appeared as happy as I had ever seen her. The visit with her grandmother completely changed her outlook and personality. One would have never guessed that she had experienced the tragedies that had plagued her.

Faith rode in the front seat the entire distance. She sang the songs that played on the CD. She also looked at me frequently and smiled. She even shared the last remaining cookies I had baked for her. At that time, there was a warmth in my heart that I had never experienced. Her happiness wore off on me. I also found myself smiling and singing. I do not recall a time that I had ever been as happy. I never knew one person could have such an impact on my heart and soul.

The weather was delightful during the drive toward Arkansas. The temperature was as pleasant as any time since I had commenced my driving career. The sun was shielded by intermittent clouds floating through the daytime sky. I thanked God for this blessing and for assisting me in eradicating the dark clouds of Faith's depression.

The trip almost began to feel like it was turning into a vacation. In Oklahoma City, we stopped at a truck stop to freshen up. Likewise, we saw a diner near this location. The diner was family-owned and operated. This restaurant reminded Faith of the business where her mother once worked.

Faith insisted that we stop.

Not wanting to upset the positive emotion occurring since the cross, I parked next to this eatery. We went in and were seated. Looking over the menu, Faith claimed that this menu looked like the menus that her mother would provide for her and Gabe when they would take their evening ventures to eat supper many years ago. Although she realized I was not Gabe, she said how grateful she was that we were together. She thanked me again for my time and inspiration. My heart started floating again. Faith ordered a country fried steak meal with mashed potatoes. Echoing her request, I decided to order the same. I started to feel a closer connection to Faith than I ever felt.

After finishing our meal, we resumed our drive toward Nashville. The miles to Fort Smith and then Little Rock passed by quickly. As we were passing a car on the freeway, Faith's voice captured my attention. In the nearby car, a little girl was in the back seat. She was motioning for me to pull my horn cord. She also had a twin sister sitting next to her. This twin was also making a motion for me to honk at them.

Honoring this request, I honked my horn for a few seconds. They responded with their hands together like they were clapping. Faith and I could only laugh at that moment. I was certain God was showing us the divine path He wanted us to go.

After driving through Little Rock, Faith mentioned she needed to talk to me. She asked if we would be stopping again in Memphis. She wanted to walk by the river again. Finally, she claimed she had important issues to discuss.

I smiled when I told her we would be spending the night there. I had the funds for a motel room if she desired. My anxiety increased when I thought about what Faith wanted to discuss with me. Yet I still had the steadfast commitment to go where God prodded me.

We arrived in Memphis a few hours before dusk. We ventured quickly to find a motel room near the river. In this room, we were able to relax. I made a couple of sandwiches from supplies I had placed in the cooler. Afterwards, Faith took a nap in one of the single beds. I successfully dozed off in a recliner next to her bed.

I was awakened by the sound of a woman's voice. It sounded similar to Miri. The words were clear. The voice told me that Faith needed me. The voice urged me to stay with her.

Faith was opening her eyes as I stared at her. The way the angle of light hit her face created the sight of the most beautiful woman I had ever seen. She inquired if anything was wrong. I could only confess I was with the one true love I had been searching for. Faith flashed a lovely smile toward me.

I told her we needed to get ready. I was anticipating another wonderful walk by the river. Faith told me she could hardly wait. I smiled and, with a nervousness in my voice, I told Faith I loved her. She could only respond with another smile.

We eventually arrived at the river. We began following the same path we walked here on our way to the cross. As we were holding hands, Faith stopped me in my tracks. It was time for another moment of truth.

Faith calmly began the conversation. Her eyes met mine. She told me that I would be delivering the load soon. Once completed, my career would necessitate an excursion to pick up another load. Although a sad look appeared on her face, she was unemotional when she declared that she did not want me to leave her side.

Faith had a concise reason for this statement. Her church needed a youth counselor. With my knowledge of scripture along with my inspirational character, I would provide a perfect fit for this position. I had come a long way in restoring Faith's soul. Faith believed I could undoubtedly help others in other types of adverse situations. It was clear Faith wanted me in this position and never wanted me to leave her.

We continued walking without an immediate response. Surprisingly, we passed the same ducks we had seen before. They were quacking cheerfully in the water. As unexpected events occurred throughout this entire adventure, another occurrence would happen that would leave me in awe.

Faith and I stared into each other's eyes. After a minute, the father duck had flown gracefully and landed on Faith's shoulder.

The mother duck began quacking loudly. Soon, the two baby ducks were quacking in unison. This chorus of sounds almost sounded like a church congregation singing a hymn. I had never experienced a sight like that in my life.

I immediately felt I knew what I had to do. Upon returning to Nashville, I would check into Faith's counseling position. Yet, at that exact moment, I felt the need to go further. I think Faith was caught off guard by what would happen next.

The romantic moment in the sparkling moonlight along the magnificent Mississippi called for me. I had found Faith, and I never wanted to lose or leave her. With tears in my eyes, I clenched Faith's hands tightly and fell to one knee. I apologized to Faith that I had no ring. I asked what felt divine and natural. I asked Faith to marry me. Without hesitation, she pulled me up and gave me a long embrace. She whispered in my ear a simple question: "As the man who has inspired me so much, how can I say no?" At that moment, I knew I would never be without my Faith.

My Marriage to Faith

Filled with excitement, I pulled my phone from my pocket. While holding Faith with my left arm, I called Charles and Sarah. I wanted Faith's parents to hear the news. Most importantly, I wanted their blessing at the tremendous steps I would be taking in my life. Her parents meant the world to me since they initially helped provide meaning to the direction my life would take.

Sarah answered the phone. She inquired as to Faith's condition. I mentioned both encounters at the cross. Faith had experienced such a rapid improvement. Her depression was completely gone. She had been laughing and smiling again. I stated that God had cast His hand and created a blessing after an arduous inspirational fight.

Sarah was speechless and in tears. Charles came on the line. I conveyed the same information. In a calm tone, he told me he never had any doubts about my presence with Faith. He thanked me for being the angel in his family's life.

I humbly accepted the gratitude. However, I interrupted Charles and told him something very important. I needed to ask him a question. With silence on the other end, I told Charles about Faith and how I had been pulled to her during the time I was getting to know her. I wanted to spend the rest of my life making her happy. I asked Charles if I could have Faith's hand in holy matrimony. I required his blessing. In my heart, I had no doubt what Charles would say.

Charles placed the call on his speakerphone for Sarah to hear. He asked me to repeat what I had just asked. Upon repeating my words, I heard Sarah exude positive exclamations. Charles finally answered that the response I was hearing ought to provide my answer. He would be proud to call me his son. They would see us when we arrived in Nashville.

Upon returning the load to Nashville, I looked into the counseling job. Without hesitation, the church board and the pastor wanted me aboard as their youth counselor. With what they knew about Faith and her condition, I was able to work miracles. As a result, I eventually returned my truck to Sunshine Logistics. My truck driving hiatus had served its divine purpose.

After a year living and working in Nashville, Faith and I finally got married. It was a modest-sized wedding with mainly Faith's family present. On that special day, Faith was happier than I had ever seen her. While she did not specifically say these words, Faith was content to be restored to her simple life with her simple family.

Shortly after our marriage, Faith asked me an important question. She wanted to try to have another family with me. Supplying the inspiration, I told her that I loved her, and God would always be there for us. However, I felt it was time for me to have my own children. She was overjoyed when I responded positively. I even mentioned what God says in Genesis 1:28: Be fruitful and multiply. Faith hugged me tightly upon hearing this response.

After our wedding, Faith and I purchased a little plot of land close to her parents. On this land, I had placed a small, simple trailer. Faith and I understood that our relationship, and not extravagance, would make us happy. One day, as I was cutting firewood for the wood-burning stove in this trailer, Faith approached me with some lemonade. She asked me to take a break. She had some very important news for me. Upon wiping sweat from my brow, I took the lemonade and sat next to her on our porch swing. I was not prepared for the news she was about to convey.

Faith mentioned that we would be having company soon. I lifted my eyes in a way that would manifest my bewilderment. Who would be coming to visit us? Her parents? Members of the church congregation? Silence was in the air for the longest time. At that moment, Faith exclaimed that she was pregnant.

For us, this had to be the most joyous moment in our relationship. Faith would be having a baby again.

A Simple Life with Faith and Our Two Daughters

Faith was overjoyed with the prospect of having a family again. Her heart was riddled with a nervous anticipation at this prospect. I reassured her that God would play a vital role in our lives. He would provide similar blessings like Faith experienced at the cross. Grasping the locket she still wore around her neck, Faith displayed comfort on hearing these words. Great things would begin to happen to her and her family.

Prior to the birth of this child, I received a promotion. The church pastor was impressed at the progress I was making with youth issues, so he asked me if I was interested in becoming the associate pastor. I was humbled and flattered at that request. Without hesitation, I accepted this invitation. God was pulling me even closer to Him.

After a smooth and uneventful pregnancy, Faith gave birth to a little baby girl. This baby had her mother's looks and a sweet aura rarely seen in babies that small. We decided on a precious name for this child: Hope Eliza. Before long, Hope became the apple of Faith's eye. Her simple life with a simple family had returned with a vengeance. God began to play an even greater role in our lives.

Several months after Hope was born, the church pastor decided to retire. He had an unforeseen offer for me. With some additional training, he wanted to turn over the reins of the congregation to me. He asked me if I had an interest. He told me how I was now doing more for the whole congregation than merely the disadvantaged youth. I was excited about this prospect. The feeling of being called by God was truly a feeling like no other.

I returned home to give Faith the news. As she was holding Hope, she also had some important news. I told her she should go first. I was ecstatic when she said she was pregnant again. I rushed to her with tears and embraced her and Hope for the longest time. Our lives were continuing to come together as part of God's plan.

Any news I had felt anticlimactic. However, I told her of the pastor's proposition. Faith squeezed me tightly. She could only say that I deserved it, and she continued to be so proud of me. We told each other how much we loved the other, as Faith continued holding Hope. Looking down at this precious baby girl, a smile overtook her face. No amount of gold could approximate the feeling I possessed at that moment.

After another uneventful pregnancy, Faith gave birth to another baby girl. We named this girl Sarah Miranda. There were obvious meanings behind the names we picked for our two girls. Family had always been an important part of Faith's life. By choosing those names, it was almost like we had restored a piece of her lost family to life.

After persistent studies, I eventually assumed the role of pastor for my congregation. No career has ever been as rewarding as this position. I see people at their darkest hours. However, I am uplifted by the successes and joys I see each one of them experience. I could have never predicted the bright path God would direct me down.

I was sitting on our porch one day with Faith. It has been thirty years since this adventure started. From an uncertain economic climate as a lawyer, I had turned into an inspirational messenger from God. I now had a beautiful wife in Faith, along with two loving children, Hope and Sarah. I was provided direction by Miri to discover another path in my life. God would be leading me gracefully along this path. I learned never to give up when I saw a formidable obstacle. I had saved Faith's life physically. However, I also delivered her from the jaws of a depression that was determined to kill her.

Faith and I held hands that day on the porch and said a prayer. I thanked Miri for coming into my life to point me to God and Faith. Moreover, I thanked Eliza Faith for her visits and for my time getting to know her. I really thanked her for the list of bible verses and the recipe for the cookies I would frequently help Faith bake for our girls. I continue to carry that faded list in my pocket wherever I go. There remains a moral to this story. Never underestimate the power of faith and inspiration in directing one down the path God wishes you to go.

There is always light and happiness at the end of a dark tunnel.

CHAPTER 22

The Birth of the Virus

The repetitive clatter in the hospital room reverberated through the air. First, there was the more passive sound of the blood pressure cuff engaging at a distance. Shortly thereafter, one can hear the relentless beep emanating from the heart monitor. However, overshadowing those sounds were the consistent pulsating breaths associated with an operating medical ventilator. All these sounds conveyed the reality of someone struggling for their life.

A chart clipped to the end of the bed identified the patient as Ezra Ray McKinney. He had been in the hospital for a few weeks. However, Ezra had only recently been moved to intensive care. Since his initial hospitalization, his condition has progressively deteriorated. The novelty of the virus took all medical personnel by storm. There had yet to exist a clear and effective way to treat the infection.

Initial news reports conveyed that the illness in some way originated in Southeast Asia. The exact source was indeterminable. With the new presidential administration, the attempt to streamline fiscal responsibility was important. Efforts to restructure health personnel and locations, along with any pandemic response, were undertaken for two reasons: 1) the immediacy of a pandemic did not seem to exist, and 2) the number of personnel left intact due to budgetary considerations was thought to be sufficient to catch a burgeoning pestilence. How wrong the administration was!

With staffing reduced to 25% of its pre-pandemic levels, it was impossible for the remaining personnel to catch the spread of the virus. Like the volatile embers of a thriving and formidable wildfire, the contagion rapidly spread throughout Asia, then across the heart of Europe. Now the impact could be felt throughout the United States. With no effective treatment, along with its aggressive spread, death appeared imminent in serious cases, especially with those patients having preexisting health conditions. Ezra had just been at the wrong place at the wrong time.

Ezra lived in Atlanta, Georgia. He was nearly 75 years old and still in excellent health. During his life, he never developed any notable health issues. Other than an occasional complaint concerning joint pain or muscle aches, he truly epitomized a poster man for ideal health at his age. That thought was why it was so hard to accept that his health had been driven down by this nascent respiratory illness. His rapidly weakening resistance made his doctors question whether Ezra's immune system would successfully eradicate this illness.

With no effective treatment yet to be developed, the state of Georgia alone had already lost a few hundred residents in a very short time. The pandemic was not even a few months old. Many more patients had to be hospitalized with worsening conditions. Hospitals nationwide were being overrun. The disease had an incubation period of several days from the infection to the onset of discernible symptoms. Therefore, one could appear asymptomatic and spread the virus. At the initial stages, it was difficult to know who had contracted the virus. Once the disease had advanced to utilizing a ventilator, the eventual prognosis was very grim. For Ezra, it now appeared to be just a matter of time.

Ezra had been visiting with his family in Roanoke, Virginia, a few weeks prior. His son, Eben, had married his childhood sweetheart, Sarah, twenty years ago. Eben and Sarah were the proud parents of twin girls: Rachel and Amy Jo. Ezra took immense pleasure in the drive from Atlanta to Roanoke. While he loved the visits with Eben and Sarah, his heart was committed to pampering his two granddaughters. He would shower them with presents as well as drive them around to scenic places to camp, fish, or merely to picnic.

During this latest excursion, Ezra and the girls had been camping at a site near the Blue Ridge Mountains. They had heard news reports detailing the rapid emergence of the pandemic. Unfortunately, they initially did not take the relevance of a blossoming pandemic seriously. Media reports had yet to furnish health guidelines on how to mitigate the swift spread. Likewise, the administration in Washington did little to stress the severity of what was occurring. As a result, Ezra had developed a slight fever with some scratchiness in his throat the first evening of the outing.

On the second day of this camping outing, Ezra developed symptoms that began to affect his ability to function. Along with more intense intermittent fevers, he developed a serious headache accompanied by extreme body aches. Even though simple drugs like Tylenol or ibuprofen would lessen these symptoms, those conditions continued. Added to these symptoms was a general lethargy that affected his mobility. Only when Ezra began to develop a dry raspy cough with difficulty breathing did he finally make the decision to stop camping and leave Roanoke and his family.

Ezra returned the girls home, and their parents provided food and snacks for Ezra's return to Georgia. Since his cough had significantly worsened, Eben urged him to stay in Roanoke to seek medical care. Disregarding this request, Ezra felt that an effective treatment was more likely in Georgia. Both girls kissed him on his cheeks simultaneously. He then entered his truck and began the seven-hour drive to Atlanta.

While Tylenol and ibuprofen kept his condition stabilized for the journey, Ezra felt the compelling need to drive directly to the hospital. Medical personnel wearing protective masks greeted him at the entrance. They were also equipped with safety nylon gloves, sleeves, and plastic aprons. A few assistants were carrying digital thermometers. The mere sight of these individuals scurrying around in the emergency entrance clearly conveyed the gravity of the situation. The conditions were such that their presence was nothing like the country had ever experienced.

With the help of a compassionate nurse named Ann, Ezra was placed in a wheelchair and taken immediately to one of the last remaining rooms at the emergency wing of the hospital. Because of the rapid and devastating spread of the illness, the hospital had to begin utilizing areas of a parking garage as a triage to initially assess patients and discern a treatment priority. Apparently, Ezra had arrived at the right time. If he had arrived a few minutes later, the hospital would have run out of room to accommodate his illness. Upon hearing this news from Ann, Ezra began to pray.

Ezra requested that he be allowed to briefly call his family. Upon his doctor's approval, Ann dialed Eben and Sarah's phone number. Ezra spoke very briefly. He quickly detailed his condition and his presence at the hospital. He vividly described the chaotic scene he was experiencing. He asked to pray with Eben and his family. Most importantly, he wanted to convey how much he loved Eben, Sarah, but especially the twins. Before concluding the call, he talked briefly to Rachel and Amy Jo. He faintly heard Eben and Sarah cough simultaneously in the background.

After the call, a somber cloud enveloped Ezra's heart. Could his family be getting sick too? Would Rachel and Amy Jo be spared? Was this the beginning of the end of his wonderful life? One will never know his exact thoughts then as the symptoms gradually forced him to lose consciousness.

www.ingramcontent.com/pod-product-compliance
Lightning Source LLC
Chambersburg PA
CBHW020804310726
48969CB00002B/688